THEODORE BOBNOGGIN

and

THE BACKYARD CHRONICLES

BOOK TWO: THE BIG BAD

Stephen Lunn

GW00675253

For

Mom & Dad

and

Annabelle
of course

A BIOLOGICAL IMPERATIVE

A WHITE-TAILED DOE watched her young daughter walk up to the water's edge. Thirsty. She had been taught to be careful. Look first, smell the air. Scan for any movement in the water.

The Big Bad was under the surface, listening. The lapping sound of the small deer was irritating. This is my water. You cheeky fool, you are drinking without my consent? He lifted his head to reveal only his bulging eyes and snout just above the water line.

The American alligator is possessed of an overly large *medulla oblongata*, a part of its brain stem that makes them aggressive and ill-tempered. The Big Bad had a hyper-enlarged *medulla oblongata*, which is partly why he was The Big Bad. At sixteen feet and fourteen hundred pounds, he was the terror of the swamp. He would kill for the sake of killing - and kill some more, just because. He was a machine, without remorse, and would kill for no reason other than because he had to. He was compelled. It was a biological imperative.

* * *

A slow, slow drift toward the small deer. With a heavy wag of his tail, The Big Bad propelled himself out of the water with remarkable speed, clamping down on his prey with thirteen hundred pounds per square inch of bite force. The deer was pulled into the water where The Big Bad performed a death roll until his prey drowned. The Big Bad dragged the animal back to the shoreline where he spat out his kill. He wasn't hungry, he was just in a bad mood.

The mother deer watched helplessly from behind a stand of cypress trees. With liquid eyes, she turned into the cypress trees and disappeared.

SEMINOLE OF THE WIND CLAN

FERN, FIFTEEN YEARS old and trying to help make ends meet, was at the Princeton Dunes Golf Club, a half-hour bus ride from the Tampa Seminole Reservation. She wasn't playing golf. She was patrolling the out-of-bounds areas, sneaking through the brush and scrub palm trees along the edges of fairways, hunting for lost golf balls. At three or four dollars each when brand new, an asking price of a buck-a-piece was an easy sell to the golfers in the parking lot. Dr. Fitz was her best customer. She didn't know if it was Fitzgerald or Fitzpatrick, or Fitz something else, but no matter, he was a good guy. He would say that he only wanted four balls but never had any singles, only a five-dollar bill. Keep the change, Fern, he would say with a wink. It was cash for the laundry room at the two-bedroom apartment where she lived with her mother.

Near the edge of the green on the sixth hole, Fern reached into her backpack for a zip-lock baggie of sliced cucumber. She knew a particularly large green iguana was a frequent visitor and she was trying to make a new friend. Any friend would be nice. She carefully placed the cucumber along the short-cut grass and took off into the rough along the fairway. She waited. It wasn't long before the prehistoric-looking lizard waddled up, seemingly from out of nowhere, to dine on the delicacy. One of these days, she thought, she would sit near the cucumber and see if the beast would come. But not today. Friends don't come easy, if at all.

Her backpack was freighted with more than a dozen golf balls when Fern decided to call it a day, saving enough time for a stop at the library. She had made the decision to stop going to the public school and put herself on an accelerated curriculum at home, following advanced courses online. Public school was a waste of her time and she knew it, so she would simply say to anyone who might inquire (nobody) that she was being home-schooled. The library was to feed her appetite for fiction.

Fern cruised the aisles this day, with no particular title in mind before settling on John Irving. The Cider House Rules. The dust jacket said something about an orphanage, and so her decision was made. Fern wasn't an orphan but felt like one. She used the automated book checkout system so she wouldn't have to speak with anyone, and began her read on the bench at the bus stop. She read some more while on the bus and then read more again at home, not once wondering where her mother was.

At page one hundred and eighty-five, Fern heard a key in the front door. She turned out her nightstand light and listened to the sound of the refrigerator door closing, the unmistakable *pffst* of a beer can being opened, and then the television being turned on. She pretended to be sleeping, but it didn't matter. Her mother wasn't going to check in on her anyway.

Of the Wind Clan and descendant of the now-extinct Timucua people, Fern was a Seminole Indian (on her mother's side) and proud of it. The Tampa reservation was essentially a massive hotel and casino. Parking lot included. Her people lived generally nearby and just about all of them worked at the casino or hotel in one capacity or another. Her father was an itinerant construction worker from *up north* somewhere and hadn't been seen or heard from in years. Irish he was, she remembered her mother once told her, as if that would explain anything other than Fern's chlorophyll-green eyes. Didn't Doc Fitz have green eyes? Maybe he was Irish too.

 Fern's mother worked at the casino, over-serving drinks to tourists at the blackjack tables, forty-plus hours a week, and then over-serving drinks to herself when she got home. Fern had been cooking her own meals, washing her own laundry, and self-parenting since she could remember. What kind of home was this? Fern would wonder and wonder some more.

Fern walked into the kitchen to see her mother scrunch up a piece of paper in her fist and toss it into the trash.
  "What's going on?"
  "He's gone, Fern."
  "Who's gone?"
  "Your father. Who else?"

"Where did he go?"

"I have no idea, but he's not coming back this time, so don't get your hopes up."

Fern was eight years old. She cried her eyes out and got nothing from her mother. Not even a hug. She swore that someday, she too would leave. Just go - and not come back.

Getting up early to wash the golf balls she would sell later that day, Fern then launched her web browser to the advanced calculus course she was breezing through. After snacking on a peanut butter and banana sandwich, she picked up her library book, fascinated by the story of the orphan, Homer Wells. Another day. Schoolwork, lunch, reading. There must be a better place than this.

Fern continued reading at the bus stop. She was heading to the golf course and was disappointed when the bus actually arrived on schedule, cutting into her reading time. That's fine. Time to make some money. She scanned the parking lot looking for the big Mercedes Benz that belonged to Dr. Fitz. Not here. I guess he can't golf every day, Fern mused. Forty-five minutes later, Fern had sold all of her balls. With money in her pocket, she ventured back out onto the course to look for more. She would spot iguanas from time to time and smile at them. They were harmless. It was the snakes she would worry about. And, of course, the alligators in the water hazards. Stay away from the water, she would remind herself.

None of this particularly mattered a whole lot the day Fern's life was changed forever. That day when she was on the golf course and, as happens in Florida, a thunderstorm arrived out of nowhere. Fern could sense the sudden drop in barometric pressure but thought she had time. She did not. To be in the middle of a golf course in a thunderstorm is generally a bad idea, so Fern bolted across the fairway to take cover in a deeply wooded area. Too late. A blast of electrostatic malice pierced the top of her head and glued her feet to the ground before blowing off her shoes and hurling her fifteen feet, airborne, into a sand bunker.

Fern woke up sometime in the middle of the night, soaking wet, and looked up at the stars. A billion stars, all winking at her, telling her it was going to be okay. So, she smiled a smile right back at the stars and closed her eyes, falling into a deep and oddly warm sleep.

Dawn arrived, failing to surprise the world yet again, and Fern, feeling just fine, thank you very much, opened her eyes to see a large green iguana staring at her. The iguana she would feed. "Hey! Jeez. Get away," she shouted, scrambling into a sitting position.

The iguana jerked its head left, then right, bird-like, as if to see if there was anybody or *anything* else in the vicinity and then replied in perfect English: "Are you talking to me?"

Fern did a double-take. What is this? She scooched back a few feet. "Umm, yeah. Are you talking to me?"

"If you are talking to me then I am talking to you," the iguana said, matter-of-factly.

Fern had the vague memory of being in a thunderstorm and then flying through the air. She felt the top of her head. It was itchy, but otherwise normal. "What happened?" Wait, why am I talking to this iguana?

"You were struck by lightning. I thought you were

dead, but apparently not."

A large black vulture floated down and landed at the edge of the sand bunker. "Is she alive?" He was addressing the iguana.

"It would seem so".

"Huh. That's interesting," the bird mused.

"You know what's really interesting? She can talk," the lizard said, "and I can understand her. I believe she can understand us both right now."

"I can!" Fern practically yelled at them. "This is madness. I can understand you both perfectly." She rubbed her eyes thinking this must be a hallucination. Had to be.

The vulture looked at the lizard and the lizard looked right back. "I told you."

Fern shook her head as if to clear the cobwebs. "What's going on here?" She stared at the Iguana and vulture, both. "Is this some kind of trick?"

"I could ask you the same," replied the vulture. "What's your name?"

"Fern."

"Well, I am pleased to meet you, Fern. My name is Delroy."

"Delroy? Really?"

"Yes. Delroy. Is that okay with you?" The bird allowed a soft edge to creep into his voice.

The Iguana jumped in. "My name is Pretty."

"Pretty what?" Fern responded.

"Pretty. That's my name, Pretty. I mean really, just look at me."

So Fern did. She stared at the big green iguana named Pretty. Straight out of Jurassic Park this thing was. "Okay.

Pretty it is. I don't want to get off to a bad start with you two. I'm sorry if I seem a little off." Fern looked around her. "Have you seen my shoes?"

Delroy, Pretty, and Fern, all three, fell into a generally pleasant conversation, their collective astonishment diminishing as they went along. Fern had never heard of such a thing, a human talking to animals. Delroy and Pretty, for their part, hadn't heard of such a thing either. But here they were, chit-chatting away is if everything was perfectly normal. Pretty expressed some concern about what other humans might think if they were to be spotted. Delroy concurred. Other humans might take Fern for a simpleton or worse. Fern thought about this for a minute. They were right.

Fern and her new friends arranged to meet again the next day. Same spot, just before dark when there wouldn't be any golfers around. Delroy and Pretty were agreeable to this as all three were anxious to learn if today's remarkable events were real and not some trick of their collective minds. Fern walked barefoot to the bus stop and made her way home, feeling strangely optimistic. She knew what she was going to do. She would leave her so-called home. Leave the mother she never saw. She was going to run.

Nothing was ever the same, ever again.

THE ROAD TRIP BEGINS

"LET'S GO!" THEODORE Bobnoggin was cheering on the group to make haste. He had his SUV loaded with all the necessities for a long trip. Plenty of dog chow for Julius, the one-eyed coyote he loved as much as any dog owner could. He had nuts and berries for the squirrels, bird seed and grapes for Geppetto, the crow, and lots of bottled water. He would plan some stops along the way to get ice cream for Copycat, the lazy ginger.

"This will be the adventure of a lifetime!" Ripley enthused. She was the gray *mommy* squirrel to her daughter, Digby, and her adopted son, Figaro, the red squirrel. "We are going to finally take that road trip to Florida and visit with Agnes."

"Where is Geppetto going to sit? I don't want to sit next to a crow for the whole trip." It was Figaro, concerning himself with the arrangements.

"We will all sit wherever Theo tells us to sit. And, we will behave." Ripley shot a look at Fig and Dig.

"I'll sit next to Copycat," Digby suggested.

Figaro cast a jealous glance at his sweetheart. "What

about me?"

"You can sit next to Julius," Digby teased.

"A coyote? You want me to sit next to a coyote?"

"Well, you are friends."

"Julius and Copycat are *besties*. They should sit next to each other."

"Stop!" Ripley was getting tired of the bickering. "Let's get a move on."

Nichole Florentine, DVM, was watching the hullabaloo from a short distance. Doc Nicky had fallen in love with all the creatures in Theo's backyard, The Theodore Bobnoggin Wildlife Sanctuary, and fawned over them as if they were her children. Construction on her animal clinic had just been completed on what used to be Agnes Tilray's property and she was up to her eyeballs in making sure it would be a success. There was some trepidation in her voice as she approached Theo. It was going to be a long drive for them, from Ashburn, Illinois all the way to Cocoa, Florida and Theo had an unusual group of travel-mates. "You be careful, Mister. Don't speed and remember to give Julius his eyedrops. He's getting old you know."

"I'll be fine. We are all good. Nothing bad will happen." Theo rolled his eyes.

"Famous last words. Don't forget the sunscreen. A Florida sun in July is not a sun to be trifled with." Nicky moved a little closer to Theo.

Theo could feel the love. "You know they are all watching, right?"

"I don't care." With that, Doc Nicky planted a warm kiss firmly on Theo's lips.

* * *

"Did you see that?"
  "I saw that!"
  "I saw it too!"
  "I saw that! I saw that!"

KEEP AN EYE ON DOC NICKY

A GREAT HORNED Owl was watching the goings on from his perch, high in an old elm tree. Hendrix knew his friends were leaving the sanctuary and the clinic. He also knew that it was his job to patrol the skies and defend the territory with his life. In Theo's absence, he would be in charge. Buster, the rabbit, and Oscar, the skunk, would be his eyes and ears. Any number of chipmunks and a group of raccoons would help. He would also rely on the tentative relationship he had established with Marcus and Evander, the twin coyotes and sons of Julius. They had dominance in the green and wooded areas of the golf course adjacent to, and just across the Sycamore Creek from the Bobnoggin Wildlife Sanctuary where Theo lived in his old house and the adjacent six acres where the Dr. Nichole Florentine Animal Clinic had recently opened its doors.

The big owl wasn't overly concerned. The coyote-with-no-name and a black heart had been vanquished the previous summer, his ambitions of ruling the alliance of animals in tatters. But he was still living and that was worth bearing in mind. It was human trespass that Hendrix would be monitoring. Humans coming to do harm on sanctuary land and humans with ill-intent who might seek to harm Doc Nicky. Not that there were any indications that might happen, but Hendrix had little faith in Humans. Except, of course, Theo and Doc Nicky, and it was Doc Nicky that Hendrix had sworn to defend while Theo was on vacation with the rest of his friends. The alliance of animals.

Hendrix went over the rules in his head, highlighting the most important of them: Don't eat Theo's tomatoes, don't eat each other, friendly (animal) visitors are welcome, defend the sanctuary against unfriendly intruders, and to protect each other at all costs. This was his mandate. Obey and enforce.

Hendrix flew down to the driveway in front of Theo's house to join the send-off. From a low branch on a red maple, he spotted Julius, the coyote whose eye he took in a long-forgotten fight some years ago. "Julius," he called gently.

Julius' ears perked as he turned to see the owl and then sauntered over closer to the maple. "We will be back before you know it. Don't even pretend you will miss us."

Hendrix had a deep respect for Julius. His friend who fought the coyote-with-no-name, his friend who had been accidentally shot by Agnes Tilray, his friend who had charged a human, an armed Karl Snell, in defense of the alliance of animals. "You are going to a strange and dangerous place far from here. Just make sure you come home safely. And keep an eye on those squirrels."

"I will." Julius paused for a beat. "And you keep an eye

on Doc Nicky."

Off they went. The big road trip. Theo and his argonauts.

THE GPS TRACKER

HERMAN SNELL WAS at his desk on the executive floor of The Precept Realty and Development Group building in Orlando. It was the CEO's office and suitably large with a massive desk and several photos decorating the walls and his credenza, each featuring Herman and any number of mid-level politicians and B-list celebrities. A local golf pro, a building commissioner at a construction site, and a television weatherman whose only job seemed to be repeating *hot with a chance of afternoon thunderstorms,* day after day. Each smiling and shaking hands and each wondering if the photo would somehow come back to haunt them. Plausible deniability. Yes, he's a donor, but I barely know the guy!

"Did you get the GPS tracker on Bobnoggin's car?" He was speaking on the phone to his son, Karl. Barking, rather.

"I did. I followed him to the grocery store and stuck it under his rear bumper. I did it last week before moving my stuff down here. And it's not a car. He traded in his old Range Rover for a new SUV. An EV."

"What the hell is an EV?"

"An electric vehicle. He got a brand-new Audi. It's gorgeous."

"I couldn't care less. Where is he?" Herman snapped at Karl. He was more concerned about where Bobnoggin wasn't.

"He's in Georgia. Heading south."

"What? Georgia?" Herman half-smiled to himself as he said the words. This is too good to be true. "What is the old fool doing in Georgia?"

"I don't know, but if I had to guess, I would say he is taking a nice long road trip down here to Florida. Probably to visit Agnes Tilray in Cocoa. Why do you care so much about his whereabouts?" Karl dared to ask.

Herman thought for a moment about how much to tell his son. His son, Karl, who had completely blown one of the company's largest deals. The Tilray and Bobnoggin parcel of land that was, ostensibly, going to be the new tennis facility for the Ashburn Golf and Country Club. Now it was some sort of sanctuary and an animal clinic. It had been Karl's moment to shine, but he didn't have it in him. He didn't have the killer instinct necessary to do whatever needed to be done. Sure, Karl was capable of being an asshole. It was in his DNA. But assholes are a dime a dozen. "Your sister is going to do what you should have done a year ago, and it is better if Bobnoggin is not around."

"Okay." Karl wasn't sure where this was leading. What the hell is he talking about?

"Be in my office tomorrow. Eight o'clock." Herman clicked off.

EYEBROWS AT BRIDGE

AGNES TILRAY SAT at a bridge table, one of many, in the card parlor at the Riverside Estates active seniors community in Cocoa, Florida. Across from her was her bridge partner for the evening, a too-young-to-be-here, Xander Khan. She watched his face as the cards were dealt and watched him some more as he sorted his hand. There it is! His *tell*. Xander had lifted his left eyebrow, just a touch, meaning he had opening points. Maybe. They weren't exactly cheating. If Xander had lifted his right eyebrow, he had nothing. If he lifted both eyebrows, he had a ton of points. But Agnes knew that everybody in the room also knew what Xander's tells were. No real advantage, right? What nobody knew, was that Xander knew what they all thought they knew. He would play with them and have a little fun, issuing false tells. Good fun with the card sharps.

After bridge, Xander would always walk Agnes home from the clubhouse and see her to her door. Which wasn't all that big a deal since Xander lived in the cottage next to Agnes. But still, he wanted to be a gentleman and Agnes appreciated it very much. This tall and thin man from Afghanistan she had grown fond of. She had been told he was a translator for the U.S. Army when there was still an American presence in his country. He had been invaluable to our troops and was one of the lucky few to have earned a visa to live out his days on U.S. soil. Agnes had lost her only son in Afghanistan. The unwinnable war in the graveyard of empires had claimed her boy. It was inevitable that she and Xander would become quick and close friends.

What Agnes didn't know was: Xander's father had been a dental surgeon, married to a Pakistani woman. As a medical professional, Dr. Khan had more money than most in Kabul, so Xander was fortunate enough to grow up watching American films on an old VHS player and had learned enough English to be conversational in the least. Dr. Khan also had access to certain drugs. Painkillers. Opioids. The kind of drugs the Taliban would want. So, the Taliban came calling. They wanted dental care for sure, but they mostly wanted the drugs. One day, the elder Khan said no. Enough. He needed the drugs for his patients. One defiled and murdered sister and a defiled and murdered mother later, Xander watched through a window as a Taliban fighter ended his father's life. With a dental drill. It took two hours and buckets of blood. There was absolutely nothing he could do. He watched, he ran, he hid. He would live with the shame, necrotizing his soul, for the rest of his days.

It didn't take much convincing for Xander Khan to become an ally of the West. So, he provided translation services for his new friends, and he learned how to shoot.

Courtesy of the Army Rangers he came to love like brothers. He grew older with them, saw some die, saw some go home, and he had saved the lives of more than a few. He learned about loyalty and would never forget his American friends. Now he was in Florida playing bridge. He also had guns and he knew how to use them.

ARE YOU SURE?

BACK AT HER apartment, Fern found her mother asleep on the sofa. TV on, sound off. In her room, Fern plotted her escape. She had seen the sun setting her whole life, over the Gulf of Mexico. The ending of days. She wanted a new beginning, so she would go east to see the sunrise. The beginning of days. If she stayed here, she knew she would become a pariah. People would see her talking to animals, and the animals talking right back. She knew she couldn't hide it for long. She would be mocked by all who knew her as the crazy girl who chatted with animals as if they were human. They would make her a *circus freak,* a tourist attraction. Look! The girl can make the animals do tricks just by speaking to them!

Fern had made her decision. She dumped a load of golf balls and her precious book out of her backpack and stuffed in an extra pair of jeans, some socks, underwear, the thin blanket from her bed, and some money she had taken from her mother's purse. In the kitchen, she grabbed all the beef jerky she could find, some bananas, a jar of peanut butter, and all the bottled water she could carry.

She almost forgot, but didn't, a baggie of sliced cucumber for iguana she hoped would be her friend. Her own sneakers gone, she took her mother's. They were too big, but not by much, so she slipped them on and with a last look at her mother on the sofa, Fern quietly left. She would not be missed for a few days and thought to herself that her mother might even be relieved that she was gone. She might even delay reporting that her daughter was missing, if at all. Fine. So be it. Off she went, off to the bus stop and onward to the golf course to recruit a travel companion.

Fern met with Pretty at the scene of the *incident* on the 17th fairway of the Princeton Dunes Golf Club. "Are you sure you want to do this?" she asked the Iguana.

Pretty tucked her dewlap under her chin and blinked, bobbing her head. "Yes, I'm sure. Are you sure?"

Fern smiled at her new lizard friend. "I'm sure. We can do this together. I need a friend."

Pretty bobbed her head some more. "Okay. Let's go before someone starts looking for you."

That might take a while, Fern thought.

Fern had mapped out their course on her smartphone. They would stay close to South Orange Avenue and take shortcuts through the wetlands and swamp and trees. When something was needed, they could find a gas station convenience store to get supplies with her *borrowed* money. It seemed like a great plan in the moment, but a fifteen-year-old can't think of everything. She hadn't planned for the phone's battery to die, and she certainly hadn't planned on getting lost in the swamp and brush.

* * *

Delroy said his goodbyes to the odd couple, promising to keep watch from above. "I'll check in with you two every now and then, but I am a busy bird. Always looking for something dead to eat. I'll follow you until I know things are well underway."

"I'm not sure what you could do to help us, but thanks," Pretty said, trying to not sound unappreciative.

"Thank you, Delroy," Fern said in the cheery voice of the hopelessly naive.

Taking a bus was out of the question. Just walking down the street was out of the question. A young girl with a loaded backpack and a three-foot-long Iguana tagging along would be a scene to be remembered. So, Fern and Pretty began their journey under the cover of brush and scrub, through the wetlands. Snakes and gators be damned. Spiders? What spiders?

DO YOUR BUSINESS

TEN MINUTES AFTER leaving a rest stop and a vehicle charging station just south of Lexington, Kentucky, Theodore Bobnoggin was feeling pretty good about their trip so far. Cruising along the interstate at a comfortable speed, taking in the scenery. Next stop: Knoxville, Tennessee.

"I have to pee." It was Digby.

"What?" Her mother sounded irritated.

"What?" Julius was definitely irritated.

Theo looked in his mirror. "Digby, seriously. We were just at a rest stop. I asked everybody who needed to go, to go."

"I'm sorry. I didn't need to go then but I do now."

"Okay. Let me find a place to pull over. Maybe a store or a gas station or something. You can run behind it and pee."

"Pee," Copycat said.

"You too?" They all said at once. Geppetto just smirked in the way only a crow can smirk.

* * *

Parked at a truck stop just off the highway, Theo said, "Okay, Digby, you and Copycat run around the back of this restaurant and do your business. Figaro and Ripley, you go with them. Try to look nonchalant. Geppetto, you fly around and keep an eye on them. I'm going inside to get some ice cream for Copycat."

"Ice cream." Copycat liked this plan.

"What about me?" Julius asked.

"Stay here." Theo offered Julius an apologetic shrug. "We can't have a coyote sniffing around the parking lot."

Julius wasn't happy about that, but he understood. Too many humans going in and out and scuffling around, to and fro. So, he stayed in the SUV and watched, with his one good eye, through the back window. The dark-tinted window that humans couldn't see in.

When Theo got back to the SUV with some ice cream and bottled water, he saw only Julius. "Where is everybody?"

"Taking their time, I guess. You know those squirrels have the attention span of..."

"Squirrels. Yeah, I know."

Theo climbed back out and looked around. Nothing. Not even Geppetto. He thought he would take the opportunity of a few minutes to check in on Doc Nicky.

Three rings. "Hi, Theo?"

"Hi, Nichole. How's everything up there?"

"Good. All good. I have Cierra working the front desk and Riley is helping me in the back."

"You know they will be back at school soon, right?"

"I know. But they are a huge help for me now, at least until I can finish hiring staff."

Cierra and Riley had begun their teen romance the previous summer. Cierra had blown out her knee at basketball practice and Riley had doted on her throughout her convalescence. Now entering their senior year of high school, Cierra was back to her old self and getting ready to entertain athletic scholarship offers once again, while Riley just wanted grades good enough to get himself into a decent college. What would happen to their relationship when she went one way and he another, was something Riley didn't want to think about. Different colleges. A long-distance relationship was fraught with peril. It weighed upon them both, so they chose to simply be happy in the moment.

"Okay." Theo paused to look out the passenger side window which had been lowered so the crew could hop/scramble/fly back in when they returned.

"Is everything okay with you?" Doc Nicky had noticed the pause in the conversation.

"Sure, yes, everything is fine." Where the hell had they all gone?

"Did you give Julius his eyedrops?"

"Aaah. Ummm."

"Theo, really, you can't forget. Once a day. That's it."

"I'll do it now. I promise."

Doc Nicky heard a crash coming from her storage room.

"Uh, Doc Nicky?" It was Riley.

"Theo, I had better get going. I think Riley needs my help. You take care and say hello to my furry friends."

"Doc Nicky says hello!" Theo pretended to pass along the greeting, speaking to the mostly empty car. "They all say hello right back!"

Julius wondered what Theo was talking about.

"Okay, Julius. I shouldn't do this, but I have to. We have to go looking for them. I know you hate *the leash* but it's the only way. I have to seem like I am walking my dog."

"Your handsome and noble dog."

"Yes. My handsome and..." Theo's sentence was truncated by the arrival of Geppetto.

"I tried to get them to hurry, but they don't listen. They never do."

"Where are they now?"

"Right here. Open the door and let them in."

Copycat climbed in first, the prospect of ice cream putting a spring in his step. The squirrels followed, wondering if they might be in trouble.

"What took you so long?" Theo tried not to sound too upset. "I thought I told you to be quick?"

"You didn't say be quick," Digby gently corrected Theo.

"She's right. You didn't say be quick," Figaro backed up his sweetheart. "The word *quick* was never spoken."

Theo sighed.

Back on the highway, they blew past Knoxville, right through Tennessee, and into Georgia. The next time they pulled over for a potty break, Theo would go with them, one at a time, while the others waited for their turn inside the big Audi.

Just past Atlanta they finally agreed upon which radio station to listen to. It had been a constant battle and the bickering behind him was driving Theo nuts. Julius wanted classical music, and Geppetto wanted NPR even though he couldn't understand a word they were saying. Ripley wanted pop music. Theo could get just about anything on his satellite radio, so, in the end, it was *yacht rock* that was unanimously declared as something they could *all* listen to. Except for Theo. He wondered if it would give him *brain mush*.

THE TALL AFGHAN

XANDER KHAN SCOOPED up his dog, Yogi, into the crook
of his elbow. The dog's name perhaps a latent memory
formed while watching American cartoons as a kid. "Let's
go puppy dog," he said to the diminutive Maltese,
resplendent in his bow-tie ribboned pompadour. "Let's
pay a visit to Agnes next door."

Tail wag.

Agnes was halfway through a bottle of drugstore wine
when Xander arrived. She could afford the good stuff, but
old habits die hard. She was in a cheerful mood already
and when Xander showed up with Yogi, that mood only
improved. His cottage and small backyard were separated
from hers by only a hedge and a small fenced enclosure he
had erected as a little-used dog run for Yogi. Both
properties backed up to a pond, fed by an estuary linked
to the intercoastal waterway of the Indian River, slicing
through Cocoa. She loved it here and she loved the view of
the mangroves across the way. She didn't love the
occasional alligator sunning at the water's edge, but they

didn't mess with her, and she didn't mess with them. It was the fat snake always curled up on a low branch of the orange Geiger tree near the water that Agnes kept a close eye on, probably for no good reason, but she did anyway.

"Hi, Yogi! Come here! Give me kisses!" Agnes put down her wine glass in preparation for Yogi to launch. And he did. Straight onto her lap and all kissy-face until a smiling Xander took the amorous canine back into his clutches.

"Hello, Agnes."

"Hi, Xander. I wasn't expecting to entertain any gentleman callers, but come on over here and gimme a hug."

He did just that, carefully, as he deposited a tray of Gosh-e fil on the patio table. It was the favorite pastry of his country and battles would be paused in order to eat it. Agnes loved it, or at least, said she did. "You seem in a good mood, Agnes."

"You're damn right I am! I just got off the phone with Theo. He will be here in the morning. And so will my beloved Fred." She looked up then added, "They call him Copycat, but I don't know why."

"That's fantastic, Agnes. I know how much you have been looking forward to their visit."

Agnes appeared lost in thought for a moment. "There is something I've been meaning to tell you." She looked at the tall Afghan and thought she saw an *oh no, what* expression fall across his face.

"It's okay. Tell me."

"Well, he has some travel companions." *Pause.* "He has three squirrels, a crow, and a coyote with him in his car. Along with Fred, of course."

"Isn't that special," volunteered Xander, wondering

how much wine Agnes had already consumed. Crow? Coyote?

"I'm not kidding, Xander. Theo is a little odd. Special, I think."

Xander nodded his head as if to say *continue.*

"Nogs thinks he can speak to animals. Really. I've seen it. He prattles away at whatever creature might come along. It looks like they are yammering right back at him. It is very strange. So, I just play along. No big deal. I don't know what else to do."

Xander could feel in his bones that Agnes was not crazy, and Theodore Bobnoggin wasn't crazy either.

"They will likely be unruly after a long trip, and I don't want Yogi to have any ill will towards them. I think we might have to keep an eye on this."

"Don't worry, Agnes. It will be fine."

Xander and Agnes enjoyed some pastries and wine together, the conversation, albeit subdued, drifting from the subject of talking animals. After a time, Xander said a respectful goodnight and, Yogi in tow, headed back to his cottage. After brushing his teeth and putting out a bowl of fresh water for his dog, he turned out his nightstand light. Unable to sleep, he thought about an old folk tale they would tell in Afghanistan. A boy from a small village just north of Mazar-i-Sharif had been struck by lightning and had lived. He awakened from a stupor amazed to be still breathing. The villagers all thought him insane because he would run around talking to the goats and chickens. He insisted the goats and chickens were talking right back to him. He was at first seen as an oddity, then as possessed. He was eventually banished from his village as a devil of some sort. They had given him nothing more than a knife and a canteen of water. A boy to be shunned. He then went to live high in the mountains. He was said to be sleeping in caves under the protection of wolves and Dzu-Teh. The Himalayan brown bears. He was seen by villagers, periodically and variously, consorting with sheep, wolves, and deer. Sometimes a striped hyena. Sometimes many. Nobody really knew how much of it was true, but the stories persisted. And those stories were believed by all who had witnessed his ramblings. These stories were passed from village to village and soon all of Afghanistan knew of the devil boy who could speak to, and control all manner of wildlife. Animals that would do his bidding and attack at his command. He was feared.

Xander believed these stories with all of his being. He *knew* them to be true.

ARE WE THERE YET?

"ARE WE THERE yet?" It had been a familiar refrain coming from the back seat ever since they crossed the Georgia-Florida state line. Every fifteen minutes it seemed.

"Almost," Theo would reply, wondering about the sensitivity of animals to the passage of time.

"I'm hungry."

"I'm thirsty."

"Put down the window."

"Put up the window."

On it went until Theo exited I-95 and announced their imminent arrival. The excitement grew in the air and in the beasts behind him. "Slow down and let me out," Geppetto requested. "I'll make the last of our trip from above. I want to do an aerial reconnaissance. I'll follow you."

"Recon!" Fig and Dig said together.

"Recon!" Copycat copied.

Theo's NAV system brought him into Riverside Estates and then to Agnes's driveway. He put his SUV in *park* and looked out at Agnes's cottage. Small, tidy, tasteful. Not bad he thought to himself. He liked it. "Okay, you guys wait here. I'll be right back, so no fooling around. I'm going in to see Agnes."

Agnes beat him to it. As Theo's door closed, Agnes's door opened. Her glee unconstrained, she fairly danced along her walkway to smother Theo in her arms. "I can't believe you're finally here!"

"Hello, Agnes! I am absolutely thrilled to see you!" Theo hugged Agnes right back, careful not to squeeze her eighty-two-year-old body too hard. "Let me get Copycat."

Geppetto was finding palm trees to be a difficult perch, so he settled on a live oak in the front yard and watched. Theo opened the back door of his Audi and, like circus clowns tumbling out of a miniature car, out came three squirrels who bolted for the same tree where Geppetto sat. Julius remained inside as he had been warned to do, and then Copycat rocketed straight for Agnes, landing in her outstretched arms.

"Fred! Oh my God, Fred!" Agnes started to cry.

The three squirrels took this all in. "She sure does love that cat," Digby offered.

"*I* love that cat," Figaro added.

"I know you do. He saved your life."

"Yeah. I remember when Julius was going to eat me, you know, before we became friends."

"I'll never forget. It was Copycat who came to your rescue."

Agnes wasn't about to let go of Copycat anytime soon, so Theo went back to see Julius. "This is going to be tricky. I'll bring you in the house and then we can scout around the backyard in a bit. We can't have the neighbors calling the cops about a coyote running around."

"Got it. But I am going to have to stretch my legs at some point," advised Julius.

"I know, Julius, hang in there. After dark I can get the leash and we can be a normal guy and his dog going for a walk."

"Normal?"

NO HUMANS

FERN AND PRETTY made good time at first. Cutting through the wetlands, trying to stick to solid ground, they would occasionally have to wade through seemingly opaque swamp water. Fern was always on the lookout for snakes, and Pretty would focus on spotting any alligators that might be lurking. At night, Fern would start a small campfire with the lighter she stole from her mother, mostly for the smoke to keep the flying insects away, but also for some warmth in the cool night air. Fern ate beef jerky and protein bars while Pretty feasted on nighttime crickets. They would not dare cross through water at night as the alligators were about and in numbers. Pretty proved herself to be an excellent swimmer and so would check the daytime waters before they would risk a crossing. Things seemed to be working out well. Until Fern ran out of drinking water.

"Let's head over closer to the road. There has to be a gas station or something where we can get some water and re-supply. If I don't get some insect repellent, those mosquitoes are going to eat me alive."

"Look up," Pretty said.

Fern did just that and saw a large black vulture overhead.

After a few lazy circles, Delroy floated down to greet his friends. "Hello, Fern!" he said with genuine enthusiasm. "Pretty, you are looking fine as always."

"Delroy!" Fern and Pretty said together.

"I've been keeping a lookout behind you. There is nobody on your trail, no *humans* anyway."

Fern stared. Concerned. "No humans. What does that mean?"

"It means there is a Mama bear with her two cubs over that way," Delroy beak-pointed. "No sign of Papa bear."

Typical, thought Fern. Bear fathers too.

"It also means there is a panther trailing you."

"A panther? We are too far north for a panther," Fern argued.

"Not this one. It looks like she is favoring a forepaw, so she might be injured. That means she is hungry and in a bad mood."

"I don't like the sounds of this," Pretty volunteered.

"She is still a distance back, but she is definitely tracking you. She's not after you, Pretty, you're too ugl… too pretty to eat. But she smells Fern."

A SPECIAL PROJECT

HERMAN SNELL STOOD behind his desk looking out the floor-to-ceiling windows in his office, watching the air traffic in and out. Planes taking off and landing at Orlando International Airport. People coming to visit a *freaking* theme park. Uncountable families willing to drop a month's pay for a once-in-a-lifetime trip to appease their screaming and entitled brats. Unreal. Buy yourself a patch of swampland for a song, put up a few roller coasters, and build a hotel. Just like that. A license to print money. How much is that cheeseburger? What? Are you kidding me? What a disgrace. He wished he had thought of it. Anyway. His son would be here soon, for whatever that was worth.

Karl Snell awakened at 5:45 as always, beating his 5:50 alarm. Push-ups, sit-ups, cottage cheese, and toast. Coffee, shower, teeth whitening strips. Discipline was the key to success! Blue suit, white shirt, and a careful tie. Time to go and see his father.

Without knocking, Marcy Dingle entered Herman's office

at 7:58 a.m. and considered her boss for a few moments before speaking. There he stood, hands clasped behind his back, just staring out the window into space. He looked a bit like Shrek. Stocky, large head, no neck. In fact, he looked a lot like Shrek, except not green. Marcy smiled to herself, wondering why this hadn't occurred to her before now. She cleared her throat before disturbing Herman's window-gazing reverie. "Your son is here, Mr. Snell." Marcy had worked for Herman for years and knew all the ins and outs. All the internal machinations. She hadn't a care in the world as far as her job was concerned. She knew enough to absolutely *bury* the Precept Realty and Development Group. She was untouchable. Herman couldn't fire her. Ever. She liked that.

"Why are you wearing a tie?" Herman looked at his son in amazement.

"I, uhh, I don't know. I wanted to be respectful?"

"It's Florida. It's July. You look like some idiot from *up north.*"

I *am* from up north, Karl thought briefly, before wishing his father would just hurry up and have a heart attack and get it over with. "Okay, sorry."

"Take off that tie and let me see it."

Karl loosened, then removed his necktie. "Here," he said, handing it to his father.

Herman examined the tie carefully, appreciating the material. He turned it over to look at the label. Zegna. With a gentle nod of approval, he muttered, "I'm paying you too much." He gently folded the tie and put it in his desk drawer. A confiscation to confirm status. "Sit down, Karl."

Karl sat.

"Where is he now? Bobnoggin. Where is he?"

"Cocoa. He is staying at Agnes Tilray's place. I did a drive-by. He, umm, brought some of his animal friends."

"He really is nuts, isn't he? Talking animals."

"I think so. Full-on crazy," Karl concurred.

"He might be crazy, Karl, but he outsmarted you, didn't he?"

He outsmarted everybody, thought Karl. Bobnoggin had snookered them all, buying the Tilray property from Agnes before the Precept Realty and Development Group could close on the deal they thought they had. Agnes's land, combined with his own, gave Bobnoggin the extra leverage he needed to tell Precept and the Ashburn Golf and Country Club to shove it.

"Are you all settled in, Karl? At your new condo?"

"Yes, thanks. I still have boxes all about the place, I'm still unpacking some things. It's only been a few days, but I'm getting there."

"Okay, good. Your sister has moved into your old place up in Illinois. I imagine *she* has finished unpacking. Gerda has some important work to do. She is keeping control of the Northeast and assuming responsibility for your old territory in the Midwest. I want you working here with me in Florida." Herman locked eyes with Karl. Don't you dare complain, kid.

"I understand," Karl said. Actually, he didn't, but that's fine. He would be closer to the seat of power in Orlando, he would have his father's ear and he would win back his trust. "What is it exactly that you want me working on here?"

"We have that Cuban chicken franchise looking to expand all up the coast. Miami to Jacksonville and everything in between. Pollo Cubano has a location operating in Fort Pierce right now, and another one in Melbourne. I want you to check them out. Take photos, look at aerial footage, especially during the lunch rush. Ingress, egress, traffic lights, everything. I don't want mistakes. These potential new locations are going to have to be the right size, have the best traffic counts, and they have to be able to accommodate a drive-through. No drive-through - no chance. Are you listening to me, Karl?"

Karl was indeed listening. Listening and doing math in his head. "I want to have an idea about the scope. What kind of numbers are we looking at?"

"There are over seven hundred McDonald's restaurants in Florida. Think about that."

Karl's head could barely handle the math. He could see this project taking years. Many years and a *lot* of money. Maybe he could get that Porsche that he always wanted after all. "I can do this. I'll get started right away. Is there anything else I can do?"

Herman smirked. "I might have a special project for you once in a while." He was thinking about the *special project* Gerda was going to handle for him in Illinois.

Karl stood to leave. "I almost forgot to ask. Why are you so concerned about where Bobnoggin is?"

"I don't care where he is, Karl. Haven't you figured this out yet? It doesn't matter where he is, as long as he's not at home. All the way down here in Florida is perfect. Gerda has work to do and I don't want problems."

"Okay. I'm still not sure..."

"Stop talking, Karl." Herman had had enough. "She is going to do the work you didn't have the stomach for. Now ask Marcy to take you down to the third floor. She'll introduce you to Lucia in HR and get you set up with an office."

FIRST-AID KIT

FERN AND PRETTY crept across a patch of dry land in the back of a roadside gas station. They had followed Delroy, who had scouted ahead to find a suitable place for them to re-supply. It had taken several hours in a blazing sun to find it and Fern was desperately thirsty by the time they got there. They took a few minutes to watch the human traffic going in and out of the attached convenience store. Counting. One in, two out, two more in, one out, another one out. Once satisfied that the store was probably empty, she retrieved some money from her backpack and jammed it into the pocket of her jeans.

"You stay here," Fern instructed Pretty. "I'll be right back."

Pretty stayed behind with the backpack, hiding in a thicket, and wondering how long *be right back* meant.

Inside the convenience store, Fern did her best to act nonchalant. Doopty-doopty-doo. She grabbed some bottled water from a refrigerated cooler, a can of fly spray, and then a fistful of protein bars and some beef jerky at the register. Original flavor and some teriyaki.

"That it?" It was the wholly disinterested man behind the counter. He had barely looked up from the phone he was playing with.

"No, actually I was wondering if you had a small first-aid kit. Maybe something with band-aids and antibiotic cream?"

"Right over there," the man said, pointing.

After paying with her mother's money, Fern grabbed her two plastic bags of *stuff,* and then, after making sure the coast was clear, she ducked around to the back of the store. There she met a dutiful Pretty, still jealously guarding the backpack against imaginary thieves.

"Did you get everything you need?"

"I did." Fern was chugging down some water. "I got a first-aid kit too, in case any of these bug bites get infected."

"All right, let's get out of here."

"Hang on a second." Fern proceeded to arrange her purchases inside her backpack, and once satisfied, said, "Okay, we're good. Let's go."

Together they traipsed back into the unknown, through straw-colored tall grass and brush, across some shallow water, and into a section of slash pine. Always moving east, to the place where the sun would rise and days would begin.

REALLY BIG

KARL WANTED TO check out the Pollo Cubano location in Melbourne but could not resist a quick morning drive past the Tilray cottage in Riverside Estates. It had become an obsession for him. It fueled his hatred and he enjoyed that. It gave him meaning. A slow roll past, looking out the window of his big, black BMW that he had driven down from Illinois.

There was Bobnoggin's Audi in the driveway. Bastards. Bobnoggin and Tilray. They had screwed everything up. His plans, his ambitions. Karl wanted nothing more than revenge. To inflict a little pain. To cause a *problem* for them.

Past the cottage, outside the boundaries of Riverside Estates, and going south on US-1, Karl called his sister. What was she up to with this *special project of hers?* He wanted to know.

Gerda Snell was at her desk in what used to be Karl's office in Ashburn, Illinois. Her feet were resting, ankles crossed, on the desk. She was plotting her mission when her cell phone vibrated, and she looked at the caller ID. It read: "Loser." What does Karl want? Gerda needed to think about this for a moment, so she let it go to voice mail. She knew Karl hated it when she didn't answer right away, so that was a bonus.

How are you supposed to do business if you don't answer your phone? Karl fumed. Then the speakers in his BMW chirped. Incoming call. His caller ID read: "Bitch."

"What?"

"You called; I'm calling you back."

"Hello, Gerda. I hope you are enjoying my condo and my office."

"Of course I am. I am very much enjoying *my* condo and *my* office."

"Don't be smug. I'm doing just fine down here, thank you very much. What is this project Dad has you working on up there?"

"If he wanted you to know, he would have told you. What are you working on down there?"

Karl wasn't sure how much to tell her but could not resist throwing a dart at his sister. "It's big. Really big."

"Tell me," Gerda goaded.

"We have a numbered trust set up with a shell company in Panama. Not that it is any of your business. That trust will be buying land. A lot of land. Premium locations. And, then we are going to flip them."

"To whom?"

"We already have a buyer. A chain of Cuban restaurants."

Gerda smiled to herself. "You are kidding yourself, Karl. Father is feeding you crap. He has you on a fool's errand because he doesn't know what else to do with you. You have a regular paycheck because *Daddy* gave you a job. You are crippled with solipsism. You are so much less important than you think you are."

Karl felt the sting but would not allow Gerda the satisfaction. "And this oh-so-special project he has you working on?"

"If he wanted you to know, he would have told you."

NANCY

THEO SLEPT LIKE a rock in the tasteful and tidy guest room in Agnes's cottage home. The drive had taken a lot out of him, but after blinking open his eyes, he was anxious to begin his day and have a nice long chat with Agnes. He sat up in his bed and looked down to the side. Julius was snoring on the floor.

"Wake up, Julius! Today will be an adventure."

Julius lifted his head, looked at Theo, and put his head right back down. "Okay, okay. Just give me a moment."

Theo got dressed in climate-appropriate shorts and a golf shirt and looked out his bedroom window to the backyard. He could see Ripley and Fig and Dig skittering around, nervous, it seemed, of the water's edge. No sign of Geppetto or Copycat.

"Wakey, wakey, Julius. Let's go and see what everybody's up to."

Copycat had spent the night on a pillow on top of Agnes's bed. It was a dreamscape for him, and old memories had flooded his mind all through the night. Dreams of his old home and Agnes giving him dishes of milk. Good days.

Agnes had a few dreams of her own while she slept. Similar warm memories of days past.

The two of them got up together, anticipating the day ahead. Copycat went outside to see what his cohort was doing, and Agnes had just finished brewing a big pot of coffee when Theo and Julius made an appearance. "Good morning, Nogs! Let's take our coffee outside to the patio."

"Good morning, Agnes. That sounds like a great idea."

The morning sky was bright and clear, not yet too humid, but it was coming. Geppetto was flying in wide circles, surveying the neighborhood. He saw a solitary bird perched right on top of the roof of a house, two down from Agnes. Geppetto decided to investigate. Landing on the roof just a few feet from this very strange-looking bird, Geppetto said, "Hello."

The turkey vulture appraised her visitor for a moment. "Hello," she said.

Geppetto didn't want to seem rude or forward (as crows often are) so he refrained from commenting on the turkey vulture's appearance. He did, though, entertain a great interest in the vulture's featherless, bright red head. "My name is Geppetto. What's yours, if I may ask?"

"Nancy," was the reply. She seemed quite pleased by the crow's manners. "Where are you from, Geppetto?"

"Up north. Way up north. I came down here in a car with a human and several friends. Where are you from, Nancy?"

"I'm a local."

Geppetto wondered if this new and budding friendship might be used to his advantage. Local knowledge. The inside scoop. It's never a bad idea to have a friend in the neighborhood if you are the new kid on the block.

Geppetto chose his words carefully. "If you don't mind me asking - because we don't have any birds as beautiful as you up north - what sort of bird are you?"

If a turkey vulture could blush, Nancy would be blushing.

CAMERAS AT THE CLINIC

WITH CIERRA AT her post in the front of the clinic, Dr. Florentine was in and out of various examining rooms, administering shots for this and shots for that, to the puppies and kittens who were not enjoying their first visit to the vet. Smiling new pet owners listened attentively to dietary advice and a prescribed schedule of an unending series of check-ups.

In the storage room, Riley was looking through a bunch of boxes that had been delivered that morning. Is this the right kind? Did I order the correct cameras? Does this one go inside or outside? He scratched the top of his head and was looking around for a ladder when Doc Nicky came in.

"How's it going, Riley?"

"Okay, I think. But this is going to take a little work."

"How long? Our insurance company wants it done yesterday."

"Umm, I don't know. I have to figure out this Bluetooth thing and get all the cameras connected. We do have Wi-Fi, right?"

Doc Nicky smiled. "Yes, Riley. We got it last week."

"Good. Do you have the password?"

"Cierra has it."

Riley smiled inwardly at this. Any excuse to go up front and visit with Cierra. "All right. Well, I need to get these things installed, hook them up to the internet, and download the apps for cloud storage. All that."

"Thank you, Riley." Doc Nicky turned to leave.

"Oh, one more thing, Doc Nicky. Do we have a ladder?"

I SEE YOU

FERN AND PRETTY continued their trudge east. It started to seem as if the journey would never end. Fern was exhausted and began to wonder how she would know when she got to the place she was going. Wherever that was. East. To sunrise and beginnings.

"Pretty?" She began, fatigue in her voice.

The big green iguana, also tired, looked at Fern. "Yeah?"

"I have the feeling we will be there soon." She was trying to encourage the lizard. Her cell phone battery had died. Dead. Gone. They had no charger anyway, and no place to charge it.

"I'm worried about the panther that Delroy told us about," Fern said while slogging through tall grass and shallow water. "There is no way for us to defend ourselves."

Pretty considered this. "I'm not so sure about that. Think about it. You could talk to this panther, and she would be surprised beyond imagining."

"I don't know, Pretty. A hungry cat is a hungry cat."

"It might be our only chance," Pretty said, matter-of-factly. "You might have to talk our way out of this predicament." Then added, "Should it arise."

Fern and Pretty bedded down for the night. Pretty with a stomach full of crickets and Fern with a stomach full of Mars bars and beef jerky, although that supply was rapidly dwindling. They had a small campfire, almost burned out for the night, with just a few stick-ends burning as embers. The blanket Fern pilfered from her mother's house was not much more than a tattered rag at this point, but it did the job. Something to curl up with.

"Fern?"

"Yes, Pretty?"

"We are going to be okay, right?"

"I am a Seminole of the Wind Clan and I give you my promise." Fern knew that her genealogy had not endowed her with any special survival skills, but it sounded good and she needed to believe that just *maybe*.

Somewhat mollified, the iguana closed one eye to try to sleep.

In the darkness of a heavily clouded night, with no star shine and no moon glow, a Florida panther, yellow-eyed and with black-tipped ears, crept through the tall grass with the stealth of an evolutionary savant. Closer to the human and the lizard. Small fire. Little motion. Easy prey.

Her left forepaw was cut, her injury giving her some trouble, but she was nevertheless a ghost, preparing for a kill. She was apex and knew it.

Fern woke up with a shiver in her spine. She didn't know why, but she did. She lay motionless, listening. She heard nothing, and *nothing* meant bad news. No crickets chirping, no frogs croaking. Nothing.

The big panther, sleek and beautiful, noticed Fern stirring. Too late. The cat would feed. She stepped quietly toward the human and the creature bedded with her.

"HEY! I see you!" Fern yelled. "I see you!" She jumped to her feet.

The panther stopped in its tracks. What is this? Is she actually talking to me?

"I see you, cat. You will not eat me without a fight. Not happening."

The panther, stunned by the human speaking to her, turned and fled into the brush and cypress.

Pretty, astonished at the bravery of Fern, did not sleep another wink that night. Neither did Fern. The sounds of night came back. Crickets and frogs. The sharp bark of a screech owl. The distant grunting of a few hogs.

Morning came without further incident. Packing up and getting ready to continue their trek, Pretty cautioned, "That cat is still out there, Fern. She isn't going to quit."

"I know. We will have to face her at some point." Fern held Pretty in her gaze. "You might be right. I might have to talk our way out of this." Her voice unsure.

DANTE

AFTER COFFEE AND breakfast, Theo helped Agnes bring the dishes inside. A second cup of coffee in hand, they went back out to the patio for some idle talk and to keep an eye on Copycat and the squirrels. Julius was next to their table, feasting on dog chow, sniffing the air between each barely-chewed mouthful.

"I think I am going to wander down toward the water and see what our friends are up to," said Theo, setting down his empty coffee mug on the table.

"Don't let Fred get too close to the edge, Nogs. There will surely be a gator around who would love to eat him."

"Really?"

"Really. This is Florida. If you see water, there is an alligator in it." The last thing Agnes wanted to see was an Alligator breakfasting in her backyard. "There is also a fat snake always loafing in that geiger tree over there. I would watch out for that guy too."

"I'll be careful, Agnes."

Halfway across the yard, Copycat and the squirrels came

to meet Theo. "We want to dip our paws in the water, but we are a little nervous," Ripley said.

"Of what, exactly?"

"There is a big snake right there in that tree. We don't know if he's friendly."

"Then let's go and ask him," Theo suggested.

Down toward the tree at the water's edge, they walked. Slowly.

"Hello there, Mr. Snake. Are you friendly?" Theo said, in a genial tone.

Dante, the insouciant snake, looked at the ostensibly brave group in front of him with disdain. "Friendly? Why is a human talking to me?" Dante wondered aloud.

"Because he can, snake. That okay?" It was Figaro, of course.

Dante flickered his impressively forked tongue, tasting and smelling the air. Who does this squirrel think he is yapping to?

"Are you friendly?" Digby repeated Theo's question.

"I am a Florida cottonmouth, and I am lethal. My venom would paralyze and consume you with pain. I am the most skilled assassin in the land."

Theo looked at him and smiled. "So, you *are* friendly!"

Ripley, Fig, and Dig, all thought this was hilarious. Unflappable Theo.

"He's not a cottonmouth. He's a Southern hognose snake and he is completely harmless."

The whole group turned to the voice on a flat stone at the water's edge, where sat a large frog with skin the color and texture of a ripened Haas avocado.

"Mind your own business," Dante chastised the frog.

"He talks like he's got game, but he is not a bad snake once you get to know him."

"Introductions are in order," Theo declared. "We will be visiting here for a while, so we might as well get to know each other." Theo looked around for Copycat, but he was gone. "That cat that was here a minute ago? His name is Copycat. I believe he has gone back up to the house looking for some ice cream." Theo waved his arms around. "This is Ripley, mother to these two, Figaro and Digby. My name is Theodore Bobnoggin. Please call me Theo."

"I am happy to meet you," announced the frog. "My name is Elliot, and my pretentious friend here is Dante."

All eyes went from the frog to the snake and back to the frog.

"Hi, Elliot." Figaro thought he might like this guy. He also thought he might get to enjoy the company of the snake, having been impressed by its self-important grandiosity. "Hello to you as well, Dante."

With some reluctance, but not much, Dante said his hellos. It might be more interesting to have visitors about rather than talking to the busy-body frog all the time.

"Welcome to the neighborhood, but I want to warn you," Dante said. "I might be harmless, but there is not a speck of "nice" in a gator. You cannot trust them. If you see one, get away from the water. Do not speak to them, do not try to reason with one. Just get away or you will be eaten."

"Warning received," Theo said. "Thank you."

"Did you hear that, kids?" Ripley wanted to be sure they were paying attention. "Tell Copycat and Julius the same. Stay a safe distance from the water. Watch out for gators." She looked at Elliot and Dante. "And tell them to be nice to our new friends."

IT IS A GIFT

AFTER A LAZY lunch in Agnes's backyard, Theo had a chat with his crew. "Agnes's friend, Xander, is coming over to visit. He'll be here soon. I haven't met him yet, but if Agnes says he is a good guy, that's all I need to know."

Figaro looked at Digby who looked at Ripley who looked at Julius, and so on.

"That's fine with me," said Geppetto, who had returned from his friend-making rendezvous with Nancy. He had been regaling everyone with his story about the ugliest, but nicest, bird he had ever met. Ripley, in turn, had informed Geppetto and Julius about Dante and Elliot.

"One more thing," Theo added. "Xander has a dog. So that means I want you all on your best behavior." Theo looked squarely at Julius and then at Copycat.

"Best behavior," Copycat agreed.

"How many friends can we make in one day?" Julius grumped. "Here they come."

Ripley gave the coyote a quizzical look. "How do you know?"

"I can smell the dog."

* * *

"Hello, hello, everyone." Xander, of course, had Yogi in his arms.

"Hello, Xander, come and sit with us." Agnes motioned toward a seat at the patio table.

"Hi, I'm Theodore Bobnoggin. Agnes sometimes calls me Nogs, but Theo will do just fine." Theo stood to shake the man's hand.

Xander took the outstretched hand in a firm, confident grip. "Xander. Xander Khan. I see you have brought some friends with you."

"I have," Theo replied, then to the dog in Xander's arms: "What's your name?

What the heck is this? I just understood what that man was saying and now this guy is talking to me? "Yogi," answered the dog.

"Yogi? Well, it's nice to meet you, Yogi."

Xander hesitated for a moment. How does this guy know my dog's name? Maybe Agnes was right, he does talk to animals. After the initial shock of a talking human, Yogi seemed quite excited to have met Theo, but Xander was going to hold onto him *tightly,* until he could assess the demeanor of the animals that seemed to be surrounding him. "Perhaps you could introduce us to the rest of your friends, Theo?"

"Sure, of course. This is Ripley, mom to Figaro and Digby." Figaro bowed like a palace courtier. "This is Agnes's beloved Fred. We call him Copycat." The ginger lay motionless in a sunny spot on the patio, utterly indifferent to the proceedings. "The large crow up there in that tree is Geppetto. He is a good friend." Theo had Julius sitting like a proper house-dog at his side. "And this," he motioned, "is the bravest coyote warrior in all of Illinois.

Our loyal Julius."

"Hello, to all of you!" Xander said with genuine warmth. Then to Theo: "They don't understand me, do they?"

"Not a word. But they get the welcoming vibe."

Xander looked at all the animals, who looked right back. "I don't mean to be impolite, Theo, but is it safe for me to put Yogi down?"

"Absolutely," Agnes jumped in. "Let's have some wine!"

Theo raised his eyebrows. "It's just barely past noon, Agnes."

"So?"

Agnes produced a bottle of wine and three glasses from the kitchen and sat down at the patio table with the men. The squirrels and Julius took Yogi, all fast friends, to meet Dante and Elliot. Geppetto flew off for a "date" with Nancy, and Copycat stayed planted on the sunny patio spot that he had claimed as his personal space.

After some time in the afternoon heat, and two glasses of wine, Agnes wanted a nap. "It's not the wine, it's my age."

Xander and Theo rolled their eyes as one and then went for a ride around the neighborhood in Xander's golf cart. "Let me give you a tour, and we can talk."

Cruising around in the electric cart, a cold beer in hand, Theo took in the lay of the land. "This is a nice neighborhood. It seems quiet. Peaceful." Theo took a sip of his beer. "Agnes has settled in nicely. I'm happy for her."

"You two have known each other a long time, she tells me."

"We have. I knew her husband, Harold, pretty well also.

We were neighbors back in Illinois since forever."

Xander was quiet for a moment or two. "Let me just say it, Theo. I might as well." He glanced sideways at Theo. "Agnes claims you can," he paused for a beat, "talk to animals. And from what I can see, she is right. She says you were struck by lightning and yet you live. It beggars belief, but I believe it nonetheless."

Theo did not respond.

"It is a gift, Theo. Don't think me a doubter and I am not trying to tell you your business, but this gift is one you might not want the world to know about."

Theo took this in stride and without offense.

"I think you are not alone with this gift."

It was Theo's turn to glance over at Xander. "Not alone?"

"Are we ever alone? Are we ever the only ones? The gifted? I think not." Xander gathered himself. "Let me tell you a story about a village boy back in Afghanistan. He too was struck by lightning."

I WILL NOT HUNT YOU

FERN CRACKED HER eyes open giving them a two-fisted rub. *Am I going to make it? To the place where the sun rises?* The sun had already risen nevertheless, over a still and misty landscape, quiet and foreboding.

Pretty was up and about and scurried over to Fern. Her tone was concerned and demanding. "Fern, you need water. Food."

"We need to be safe." Fern scanned her surroundings. "That big cat will be back." She half-smiled at Pretty. "I think today will be an important day. Let's get started."

The two intrepid souls, joined forever in their journey of hardship and kinship, made ready to leave. There was a white heron, statue-still in the water in front of them. A Spoonbill was nearby, fussing in the shallows. This meant there were no gators in the immediate proximity. Fern looked at Pretty, who looked back. "C'mon. Let's go."

The heron flew away, and then the spoonbill too, as if an urgency had fallen upon them. Fern was processing this, puzzled at their sudden departure. An alligator? She turned to question Pretty and was met with the deathly still gaze of the panther they had been trying to evade.

Pretty moved slowly, protectively, to take a position next to Fern. They both stood, unmoving, less than twenty feet from the panther. One leap and it would be over.

"You speak." It was a statement, rather than a question. The panther wanted to know if she had been dreaming at their previous encounter.

Fern knew it would require an artful approach to avoid becoming a meal. "Istonko," she said to the cat in her native Seminole. "Hello."

The cat lowered its head, her eyes still locked on the girl's. What trickery is this? "Istonko," she replied in kind.

"My name is Fern."

"I am Nika."

"Istonko, Nika. This beautiful creature beside me is Pretty."

Pretty? That thing is not pretty. "Why are a girl and a lizard wandering around in the swamp? You are lucky to be alive."

"I realize that, Nika. And I would really like it to stay that way." She glanced down at Pretty. "So, please don't eat us."

"I am considering just that. Well, eating *you*, anyway. I wouldn't dare eat that atrocity you call Pretty." Nika had to admit to herself, the temerity of this human was on an impressive scale. "Give me a reason. Why would a hungry cat not eat you?"

This was Fern's moment. Her time. The next words out of her mouth would either be her last, or she will somehow finesse her way out of this predicament. "You are injured. I can help."

Nika started a slow circle to her left. Nervous. "How do you know this?"

"A vulture told me. He's been watching over us and spotted you a few days ago. His name is Delroy."

"How is it that you can help me?"

"Pretty, drag that backpack over here, please."

Fern offered some well-received beef jerky to the panther. "Sit quietly, Nika. Give me your paw. Claws in, if you don't mind."

Nika sat, wary but compliant. Fern was awestruck by the size of the panther. "You've got a small cut on your pad."

"I'll live."

"Not if it gets infected. This is human drinking water," Fern held up a plastic bottle. "I'm going to rinse this wound. It won't hurt," she said, pouring water judiciously over the cut. "And this," Fern held up a small plastic tube she had retrieved from her first-aid kit, "is an antibiotic cream."

"What's that?"

"It is human magic. The kind of magic that will, hopefully, keep your paw from becoming infected." Fern could *feel* the big cat's breath on her face. "You're going to have to trust me."

"Clearly I am doing just that," Nika said.

After applying a generous *gob* of cream, Fern wrapped some gauze from her kit around the massive paw, using the whole roll, and then wound some medical tape, several times, over and under. "That should do it, Nika. Try to keep it dry, which I know won't be possible, and don't chew off the bandages. Give it a few days."

* * *

Fern picked up her backpack and looked at an apprehensive iguana. "We have to go, Pretty."

Nika was slow-walking in a circle, testing her newly wrapped paw. Not bad. "In which direction will you go, Fern?"

"Toward the place where the sun rises."

Nika pondered this for a beat. "There are bears and coyotes and snakes everywhere. All would do you harm. But there, in that direction," Nika pointed with her muzzle, "is The Big Bad. Be extra careful in and around water. You do not want to meet him."

Pretty and Fern exchanged quizzical looks. "Okay." The Big Bad?

"If my paw heals well, I will not hunt you. I will follow you from a distance and watch from behind."

"If I make it to where I am going, I will not hunt you with a gun and will stop any who might try." Fern smiled. She had become inexplicably fond of the panther.

Nika cat-smiled back. What gun? She had grown oddly attached to the strange human who had no fear.

A PROPER RECON MISSION

THE FRONT DOOR chimed and in walked a tall blonde with a cat cradled in her arms. Cierra James was at the front desk of the Dr. Nichole Florentine Animal Clinic and offered a warm smile to the visitor.

"Hi, how can I help you?"

"Umm, my cat," the woman said. "He's not eating and I'm worried."

"Okay, let me get Doc Nicky and we'll take a look. I'll be back in a sec. Can you fill out these forms?"

"Sure."

The tall blonde scribbled some fakery on the form she had been handed and looked around the reception area. No cameras. Just like outside in the front of the clinic. No cameras. Are these people crazy? Maybe it's because they have just opened and hadn't got around to it yet.

Thirty minutes later, the cat was diagnosed as having nothing wrong with it. Doc Nicky smiled. "He seems healthy. You might wish to consider a change in diet. Try some different types of food to see what he likes. Keep an eye on him and let me know how he's doing."

A cash payment was made for services rendered and the tall woman was on her way back to the shelter from which she obtained the cat in the first place. "I'm so sorry. Can you take him back? I didn't know my roommate was allergic."

"Good work, Reena," Gerda enthused from what used to be Karl's kitchen. "That was a proper recon mission. Well done."

Reena was lounging on the Roche Bobois sofa in Gerda's new digs. She liked it. High end. She had followed her partner from the east coast, not without some trepidation, to set up a new life in Ashburn. Two peas-in-a-pod they were. Both of the same mind. Get the job done, whatever it takes.

"It was easy," Reena replied. "Borrow a cat from a shelter, visit the clinic, take a look around, and bring the cat back to the shelter. Done."

Gerda smiled and brought two glasses of Grand Cru Chablis to take a seat on the sofa next to Reena. So far, so good.

STEP ASIDE, BOYS

MA PETTIS WAITED for her husband to leave. He was ostensibly working on a shrimp boat out of Dulac in Terrebonne Parish, but Ma knew better. Ronny was bringing home too much money for that. The bills were getting paid, gas for the truck wasn't a problem, and there was never a shortage of beer in the house. So, Ma let it go. But the biggest shrimp boat in Louisiana wasn't going to fill the suitcase in the closet with thirty-plus pounds of twenty-dollar bills. She stared right at it. All packed in there, nice and neat with rubber bands around the stacks. It was drug money that Ronny was into, and that was that. Not much more to discuss.

Ma's twin boys were suspicious as well. Things were too good money-wise. When their Pa showed up with a brand-new bass boat on a trailer the week before, they knew something was up and it made them nervous. The twins were born minutes apart, but they could not have looked more different. Ronny was a big music fan and had insisted on naming the boys Elvis and Carl. After Carl Perkins, that is. Elvis was, perhaps fittingly, overweight but handsome in his own way. Carl "Soop" Pettis had a slim build, a sharp nose, and narrow eyes. He was also *viper* quick with the eight-inch blade he always had strapped through the belt on his jeans. For Carl, everything was super. *How you doin' Carl? Super good, you?* After a while, everybody just called him *Soop*. Bayou boys, they could hunt and fish and wrangle just about any gator in the swamp. And like all bayou boys, they loved their Ma. So, when Ma wasn't happy, they weren't happy.

The twins were out front, fussing with an outboard motor, when their Pa came home unexpectedly. He pulled his truck into the drive and got out with a sour look on his already drunk face. Ma heard the crunch of tires on gravel and looked out the window. She saw Ronny walk past the boys without a word. Damn. What's he doing home? She ran back into the bedroom to put away the money she had been counting. Too late.

Ronny kicked open the bedroom door, putting a doorknob-shaped dent in the drywall. "I know'd it! I know'd it! You been snoopin' around."

Ma stood stock still. Frozen, she watched Ronny pull up the rug in front of the bed and lift some floorboards. He looked relieved. There were two more suitcases there. Fat and heavy.

"Ma, listen to me. This ain't my money. This ain't *our* money. I'm just holding it for some boys in Delacroix. These ain't good fellas. They're gonna want it back." Ronny was breathing heavily. Stressed. "Ma, get over here."

Ma Pettis started to speak and earned a backhand across the face for opening her mouth.

"You gotta listen. LISTEN TO ME! They are gonna come and this money has got to be here. You need to mind your

Goddamn business." Ronny made to smack Ma once again when he sensed another presence. Turning, he saw both Elvis and Carl in the doorway.

"Come outside, Pa. I want to talk to you." It was Elvis, and Elvis had seen enough.

Ma watched her husband go outside and then she stared back at the suitcases full of money. It was decision time. She had endured unending abuse at the quick hands of her husband and now some drug dealers were going to come looking for him. And the money. He was going to get them all killed. Now he was going to get into it with the boys. She had had enough. Time to end it.

In the dirt they called a front yard, the two boys faced their Pa. Elvis spoke first. "I don't know what you been up to and maybe I don't want to know. But the next time you smack Ma, I'm gonna have to kill you. I'm sorry Pa, but that's how it's gonna be."

The first thing that entered Ronny's mind was exactly what came out of his mouth. "Boy, I guess I didn't raise you right. Talking to your Pa like that. Maybe you need a smack yourself?"

Carl nudged Elvis, signaling him to step aside. He unsnapped the leather strap on his knife and stared at his father.

"You kidding me? Really?" Ronny was bug-eyed.

"I don't want to, Pa, but I will," Soop cautioned. "You touch Elvis or Ma, and I will slice you up, super bad."

"You keep that knife right where it is, boy, or I will take it from you and stick it in your earhole."

All three of the men *felt* a movement at the house. All three turned to see Ma coming down the steps of the porch, her Henry lever-action .22 varmint rifle in hand. She wiped some blood from the side of her mouth with her sleeve. "Step aside, boys."

Elvis and Carl backed up a few paces. Ronny stared at Ma with cartoonish astonishment.

Ma made her way in between the boys and her husband before saying: "Goodbye, Ronny."

The boys watched as she unloaded eight rounds into their Pa. Six in the chest and two in the face. Ronny Pettis teetered while upright for a few seconds before dropping like a sack of low-country rice.

"What do we do now," Elvis wanted to know as he began picking up the brass casings from the rounds Ma had fired. Counting them to make sure he had all eight.

"Carl, you go with Elvis. Drag Pa into the boat and feed him to the swamp. There will be nothing left of him by morning."

Ma gathered up what she needed, including the three suitcases full of money and a fourth she found in the shed. A little over one million dollars. Cash.

The boys threw into a garbage bag whatever jeans and underwear they thought they might need, and together with their Ma, headed up to New Orleans where they traded in the truck for a late model Chevy Suburban SUV. Just like that. No regrets.

"Where are we going?"

"Florida."

Ma Pettis had their names legally changed to Pettigrew. That should work. She and her sons bought sixty-three acres in Florida, west of Cocoa and just a little southeast of

Lake Poinsett. The land was non arable and had no commercial value. Wetlands. Swamp. Still, though, with enough dry land to suit them. Perfect. They built a house, a barn, and a pair of large sheds for their boats and trailers. They got a paneled work van and had painted on the side: "Elvis and Soop" and then in smaller letters below, "Gators-Be-Gone," and a phone number beneath that. The boys had set up a business for themselves as "Gator Wranglers" capturing and releasing into the wild any nuisance alligators from the uncountable and mostly gated communities near the intercoastal area where the residents didn't want their pets chomped on by some lizard. Them boys from Delacroix would never find them.

Eight years later, Ma peered out her kitchen window as a filthy and bedraggled girl walked out of the wetlands, onto her front yard. She had a three-foot green iguana at her side.

Diesel, the three-legged Pettigrew dog, half hound of some sort, and half pit bull, was chained by a twenty-foot length to a massive truck tire. He didn't even bark. The girl walked up to Deisel and began scratching him under his chin.

"What's your name?"

"Deisel, what's yours?"

"Fern."

"What's that thing?"

"Her name is Pretty, she's my friend."

SHOPPING SPREE

"COME ON IN sweetie. Let's get you cleaned up." Ma had bolted from the house to wrap the strange girl in a clean blanket and a hug. It was sorely needed. They left Pretty outside to get to know Diesel, which seemed to be going well, albeit with the reserve of a *just-met-you* situation.

Ma Pettigrew gave Fern a bottle of water before even exchanging names and then drew a hot bath. Once Fern was gently semi-submerged and in a heavenly state, Ma went outside to speak with the boys. It was going to be what Ma said. She had seen people in need of help before, and this was one of those times. This girl was going to be welcomed. Period.

Elvis and Soop wouldn't cross Ma for anything and went along with it. A girl walked out of the swamp. Whatever. She had a three-foot iguana with her. Okay. Diesel seemed to like her - even the lizard. Oh well. Ma is the boss. Wait... this girl acted like she could talk to the iguana? And Diesel?

* * *

Bathed, hydrated, and feeling lucky to be alive, Fern introduced herself to the boys at the dinner table. Homemade lasagna, crusty bread with butter, a cold glass of milk. Bliss.

Ma had warned the boys to keep the conversation light and to not interrogate the poor girl. Let her eat and then rest. We can all talk in the morning.

After sleeping for what seemed forever, Fern blinked her eyes open. The clean sheets Ma had put on the sleeper sofa had been an unimaginable luxury. Pretty was passed out on the floor next to her. Diesel came over to nose-kiss her face. "Get up Fern, come and play with me."

Fern heard Ma bellowing from the kitchen. "Breakfast!"

After the table had been cleared and the dishes loaded into the washer, Ma rummaged through her bedroom drawers and closet for some shorts or maybe a t-shirt that might approximate a decent fit for Fern. Some luck, but not much. Back downstairs, Ma grabbed the keyfob for her pick-up truck from a hook by the front door.

"Let's go," Ma said. "We got to get you some clothes."

"Where are we going?" Fern's face brightened.

"Walmart," Ma said with glee. She'd never had a girl to take care of before. This was going to be epic.

"C'mon Fern. Don't be shy. It's what you call a shopping spree!" They filled their shopping cart with jeans and tops and hoodies and t-shirts - all the things Ma figured a kid would wear these days. "Let's go and find a changing room."

* * *

Ma stood outside the dressing room looking at the time on her cell phone. For the third time in ten minutes she shouted, "Fern? Fern? What's taking you so long? Do they fit or not?" *Pause.* "Seriously? What are you doing?" How does anything take this long?

Socks, underwear. Shoe Department: Sneakers, sandals, flip-flops, waterproof boots. Health and Beauty: Shampoo, conditioner, hairbrush, toothbrush, and some girl stuff. Lip gloss, for god knows what reason. It was, indeed, epic. Ma was born again. Boys are a pain in the ass.

On the way home they stopped for burgers and fries and gorged on lunch while sitting in the truck, listening to country music. They were not supposed to eat inside the truck but did anyway. Rules be damned.

Fern amused herself that same afternoon by putting on a fashion show in front of the full-length mirror in Ma's bedroom. At the dinner table, Elvis and Soop didn't say much at first. They couldn't quite believe what they had witnessed these last couple of days. This girl who seemed to be talking to animals. Diesel apparently loved her, and that big iguana, laughably named Pretty, seemed to chit-chat away with Fern whenever she was around. It was the oddest thing.

Two weeks later. "Elvis? Carl? Don't you boys want to ask Fern something?" Ma was prompting her sons.

"Well, Fern," Elvis began while motioning toward his brother with a dinner fork, "Me and Soop have been thinking." He looked at his mother. "Ma too. We have all been thinking." Open mouth, insert fork, chew, swallow, a gulp of Mountain Dew. "We've been thinking that since you are so good with animals, talking to them or whatever, that maybe you want a job?"

"A job?"

"Yeah, a job. Maybe you want to come to work with me and Soop?"

Fern gave this less than a second of thought. Big smile. "Absolutely!"

Ma exhaled. Elvis grinned. Soop was delighted. "That's super good. We were hoping you would say yes." Soop paused to deliberate for a moment. "But we ain't going to paint your name on the truck."

Fern closed her eyes, lying on the pull-out sofa with Pretty at the foot. Was she home? The place where the sun comes up? The place to start again?

THE BIG BAD

GEPPETTO FOUND NANCY perched on the same rooftop where he had met her before. "Hello, Nancy," all nonchalant, and fake-surprised to see her there.

Hello, Geppetto!" Nancy was quite pleased to see her pal, the crow. "How are you adjusting to this warm weather?"

"You know what? It's pretty hot back in Illinois this time of year. Not so different."

Nancy took this in. The two of them performed bird head movements, back and forth, herky-jerky, up and down. Tra-la-la.

"You see that bunch of miscreants over there?" Geppetto was watching the squirrels dancing around Agnes's backyard. "That's my crew."

"Well, your crew had better be careful if they get too close to the water."

"They have been warned, believe me."

Another pause with beaks bouncing around.

"You see those guys over there? With that truck and trailer?" Nancy head-motioned toward the Gators-Be-

Gone van.

"I do."

"They are looking for The Big Bad." Nancy was matter-of-fact with her words.

"The Big Bad?"

"Yeah, The Big Bad. He is a gator of ill-repute to be sure."

"What's his name?" Geppetto inquired.

"Nobody knows. He has no name. We just call him "The Big Bad" because he is *Big,* and he is *Bad.*"

A shiver ran through Geppetto as he was reminded of the coyote-with-no-name back in Illinois. The coyote who had faced off against Julius. The big and bad coyote who lost. "Why are they looking for him?"

"Someone's chihuahua was gobbled up by a gator last week. So, anytime something like that happens, it is always assumed that The Big Bad did it. And the legend grows."

Geppetto understood only too well. An unwelcome fear grew within him. "Do you think these guys will catch him?"

"No. He is not here." Nancy turned to hold Geppetto's eyes. "He is not here, but he is not far. He is that way, toward where the sun sets." She pointed her beak. "Not far."

THEY WILL WEAPONIZE YOU

THEO ROUNDED UP all the beasts and gave them very clear instructions. Don't go near the water. Agnes was wrapping up the dishes in the kitchen after they had feasted on pulled pork sandwiches with coleslaw and pickles. And wine.

Theo and Xander had planned to take the "dogs" for a walk. It was after dark and safe for a leashed Julius to stretch his legs with his new pal, Yogi. After an extended, and thoroughly intimate, sniffing of each other's behinds, they were now inseparable.

Agnes watched the two men get ready to leave and felt a pang of jealousy. Jealous in that Xander didn't seem to care about her close relationship with Theo, and Theo didn't seem to mind at all about her new friendship with Xander. Oh, well. Men.

"You see these guys packing up over here?" Xander pointed to two men and what looked like a teenage girl, loading equipment into a work van and the attendant flatbed trailer hitched behind it. "They are around here a lot."

Theo looked at the van with the side painted: "Elvis and Soop, Gators-Be-Gone." What are they doing?

"It looks like they are done for the day, but someone's dog got taken by an alligator last week. Whenever anybody even thinks they see a large gator, they call the homeowners association. The association then thinks a lawsuit might be in the offing if they do nothing, so they call these guys."

"To catch the gator?"

"Yup. There is talk of a monster gator out there somewhere. Everybody calls him 'The Big Bad'."

"The Big Bad," Theo repeated.

"Yeah. Sometimes I think these "Gators-Be-Gone" guys perpetuate the myth, just for the business. At other times, I think they believe it themselves. They want to be the ones who catch him. The dragon slayers. They probably think there is a reality TV series in it for them somehow. Who knows?"

"It would be a great story if they did. You know, catch him. The Big Bad." Theo was smiling to himself as he said it.

The two men walked in silence for a time. Xander cleared his throat. "You know, Theo," he started, "*Big and bad* will mean different things to different people. Where I come from there is always *bigger and badder*. Just when you think you have met him, you realize that *biggest and baddest* is still out there. Maybe we all have a little bad that lives inside of us. Some more than others, I think. Just keep in mind that all monsters fear something. Even The Big Bad knows he is not immortal."

Theo wondered for a moment just how much *bad* was lurking within Xander, and then dismissed the thought. "I think I know what you mean."

"I'm not sure you do," Xander said with a gentle shake of his head. "With respect, Theo," was the afterthought.

Why is that? Where is he going with this? Theo was a trifle bewildered.

"What I want to tell you, Theo, is..." Xander gathered himself. "I think you might want to keep a low profile."

"A low profile?"

"Yes. You should know that I am still, technically, a federal employee. The U.S. government. They pay my bills and mostly leave me alone. But every now and then my phone rings and I have to answer it. Theo..." A long pause. "Sometimes they need me to do *things* for them. Things I can't talk about, but I have a certain skill set they find useful from time to time. Sometimes they need me to be somebody's *Big Bad*." Xander indulged in a sip of his beer and turned to face Theo directly. "If I know about you and your *skill set,* and I know about the boy in Afghanistan, then that is two. Why not three? Why not many? How many have your particular skill set? Certain people will want to know."

Theo felt as if he had fallen asleep and woke up in the middle of a spy movie. Where the hell was this going?

"You have my silence, Theo. But if the Chinese government finds out about you? If the Russian government finds out about you?"

"What about them?"

Another long pause. "Right now, your primary concern is our own government. The CIA, the FBI, the Department of Defense. Everybody."

Theo could not wrap his head around what was being said to him.

"You can be inserted just about anywhere in the world

with the proper training. Your skills make you a major asset and they will do *anything* to harness that. Anything necessary. Do you understand me?"

"NO, I do not!"

"You can talk to animals, Theo. They will *weaponize* you." Xander gave Theo a hard stare. "I know what it is to be weaponized. You won't like it."

MISS YOU TOO

THEO BRUSHED HIS teeth like a good soldier. He had the squirrels all settled in on the back patio, Geppetto was wherever, and Julius was already sound asleep at the foot of his bed. Copycat, of course, was with Agnes.

Looking in the bathroom mirror, he thought about what Xander had said to him. His reality had become... wrinkled. He felt ungrounded and out of sorts. *Weaponized*?

He slipped under the bed covers and felt a need to talk with Nicky.

Doc Nicky answered on the first ring. "Hi, Theo," was the warm greeting.

"Hi, Nicky. All, umm, good over there?"

"Yes, all good. You sound... off. Are you okay?"

"Yeah, I'm fine." Changing the subject, Theo continued, "How are those two kids doing at the clinic?"

"Cierra is amazing. She's a smart kid, a short learning curve with just about everything."

"What about Riley?"

Nicky laughed. "Riley is Riley. But he is a huge help and he dotes on Cierra. It is sort of amusing to watch. I like it. The two lovebirds."

"That's great news. Have you seen any of our animal alliance around?"

"No, it's been quiet in your backyard. I see Hendrix occasionally. Just flying around and hooting. He is taking his temporary command quite seriously, it seems."

"No news is good news on that front," Theo said. After a short silence he ventured, "I miss you."

"Miss you too." Doc Nicky whispered into her phone.

GAS CANS

GERDA AND REENA hopped into their Mercedes Benz coupe and took a drive to Stanton, Illinois, a pleasant one-hour trip from Ashburn. Far enough, but not too far. In the Home Depot parking lot, they reviewed their shopping list: Two red plastic, five-gallon gas cans, some cleaning rags, a respirator mask, disposable nitrile gloves, barbecue lighter fluid, a butane lighter wand, and a small package of contractor-grade garbage bags. They both went inside wearing black covid masks to cover their faces. Gerda paid with cash.

At the nearest Target store, they bought a cheap pair of sneakers for Gerda - intentionally two sizes too big - a dark sweatshirt, a pair of house-brand jeans, a black backpack, and a Chicago White Sox ball cap. Gerda paid with cash.

That should do it. They were stocked and ready. They would buy gasoline on *the day of the deed.*

Driving home, they channel-hopped on the satellite radio, Gerda thinking about how lucky she was to have a partner such as Reena. Someone who knew all about the rules and when to break them. A girl who would be okay with *certain aspects* of her job. Someone with whom she could envision spending a lot of time.

Reena was similarly lost in thought. She considered how lucky she was to have a rich girlfriend who would buy her things. A girl who was convenient for the moment. A girl that she could blackmail anytime she wanted. And, given what they were about to do, a girl she would happily bail out on if it should ever come to that. But it won't. Will it?

A CUBAN CHICKEN JOINT

KARL DID A slow cruise past Agnes's house and stared at
Theo's Audi in the driveway. They don't seem to go out
much, he mused. Maybe it's because of all those creatures
he drags around with him all the time.

Past the house, just a few hundred yards away, was the
same van he had seen recently. He lowered his sunglasses.
Gators-Be-Gone. Whatever that means. Like, they can all
be gone. Whatever. He picked up a little speed and took off,
out of Riverside Estates and on to his next stop. Some
vacant land in Rockledge. Maybe it would be a good spot
for a Cuban chicken joint. Probably not. If it's vacant, it's
vacant for a reason, but he would check it out anyway.

Moving north on U.S.1 he thought about calling his sister
to see what she was up to but decided against it. For now,
at least. He was itching to know what her *special project*
was all about. She will spill the proverbial beans
eventually. Stuck-up bitch. He would wheedle it out of
her. He just had to know.

WE HAVE TO HIDE

"HEY, COPYCAT. WHERE are you going?" Julius wanted to know. "You are supposed to stay here in the yard."

Copycat ignored the nosy coyote. He had been watching a small lizard scooting around the patio and he wanted his cat paws on that thing, *so bad.* Every time he approached it, the quick little monster would zoom this way and that. All Copycat wanted to do was play. The more frustrated he became, the more determined he was. Trying to catch him was a challenge to be sure, but Copycat was no quitter.

The little lizard zinged around the side of the house. Copycat went with him.

Julius grew agitated at the whole affair and went after Copycat. "Hey, seriously, are you chasing him?"

"Chasing him," Copycat answered.

"Get back here, now!"

Two houses away from Agnes, and one house away from Xander, Elvis and Soop packed up their gator-catching gear and threw it into the back of their work van. Finished for the day. Fern secured the equipment they kept on the open-top utility trailer they had hitched to the van. A large canvas tarp, some bungee cords, and a length of heavy-duty, grade-120 chain. The chain that would be used to secure an alligator on the flatbed if they caught one. A gator soon to be relocated in the wild and far enough from the nervous members of the homeowners association.

Fern hopped in the van with the boys, and they started away. But not before the tiny lizard scooted up onto the trailer. Copycat was hot on the trail and jumped onto the trailer after him.

I got you now! The lizard darted around as if possessed and hell-bent on a self-inflicted concussion, banging off the sides of the trailer. Like one of the three blind mice being chased by the farmer's wife with a carving knife. Copycat was too focused to notice the van starting to move, pulling the trailer with it.

"Copycat!" Julius yelled. "Copycat!"

The one-eyed coyote had only one second to think. In the end, the decision was preordained. There was no viable option for Julius. He ran at full speed, barely managing to jump up onto the trailer. He would follow and protect his friend wherever fate may lead them.

"What is wrong with you, you crazy cat?"

Copycat smiled. He had the lizard under a paw and was exceedingly proud of himself.

The van reached the main road and picked up speed.

"Where are we going," Julius wondered aloud.

Copycat looked around and lifted his paw off the lizard. Nervous now. "Where are we going?"

Following behind the Pettigrew van and trailer was an

aging Lexus with New Jersey plates.

"Norma?"

"Yes, Leo?" Norma looked up from her e-reader.

"Does that look like a coyote on that trailer in front of us?"

"Huh. I suppose it does. It looks like there is a cat with him."

Leo kept driving. "I'm sure it's just a dog."

"Has to be."

"We have to hide, Copycat." Julius was trying to remain calm.

"Hide."

"Here let's get under this tarp. The people in that car behind us are staring."

Julius pulled at the tarp with his teeth, making room to duck under with Copycat. The coyote and the ginger, trucking off to parts unknown.

WHOLESALE PANIC

WHOLESALE PANIC FELL upon the backyard where Theo and Agnes were frantically searching for Julius and Copycat.

"Where is Julius? Where is Copycat?" Theo was shouting at nobody in particular.

"Fred! Fred!" Agnes was beside herself. She ran inside the house, tearing around from room to room. "Fred! Fred!" He was nowhere to be found, so she ran back out to the backyard. "He's not inside."

Theo didn't know what to do. Then he looked at the water. Then he looked at Agnes, who looked at him. Together they ran to the water's edge. Staring.

"Oh, my God! An alligator ate Fred!"

"Calm down, Agnes. There is no way. We will find him."

"An alligator ate Fred!"

"Agnes, you need to calm down. An alligator did not eat Copycat. Not if Julius was with him. No way." Theo's mind, with a will of its own, turned to the conversation he'd had with Xander. There is no way. Unless it was The

Big Bad.

Xander heard the shouting from inside his house. "Yogi. Come with me." The man and dog both raced over to Agnes's backyard. "What's going on?

Theo called for Ripley, Fig, and Dig, who were up in a tree doing mostly nothing. They scampered down to Theo, alarmed at the tenor of his voice.

"What's happening?" It was Ripley.

"Julius and Copycat are missing." Theo was moderating his voice so to avoid panicking the squirrels. "Have you seen them? When was the last time you saw them."

The three squirrels just shrugged. "It was a while ago," Figaro said. "I thought they were napping on the patio."

"Go and check with Dante and Elliot. See if they were anywhere near the water."

Figaro didn't have to be told twice.

Geppetto was holding court with Nancy, captivating her with colorfully embellished stories about the vanquishing of the coyote-with-no-name, when he noticed a flurry of activity in Agnes's backyard. "Something's not right, Nancy."

Nancy followed Geppetto's gaze to Agnes's yard. "Something's up," the vulture agreed.

"I don't like this. Something is wrong." Geppetto took wing and rocketed to the crew gathered in the yard.

"Dante, have you seen Julius or Copycat? Elliot, have you?" Figaro wanted to know.

"No, not since this morning," Dante replied for them

both.

"They are missing. Have they been near the water?" Figaro was breathless.

"No. Not that I noticed, and I would have noticed," the snake said.

Agnes was in tears. Xander put his arm around her, looked down at his dog, and then up at his new friend. "Theo, I need you to do something. I need you to talk to Yogi."

"Yogi?"

"Yes, Yogi. Be very clear. Tell him we need a scent. Julius and Copycat. He won't necessarily know the cat, but he will know Julius for sure."

Theo crouched down to eye level with Yogi and explained the situation. "Follow the scent. Find Julius for me. He must be here somewhere. He'll be with the cat. Follow the trail, Yogi."

"Got it."

Yogi began sniffing around the patio, left then right, his nose twitching frenetically. He moved to the side of the house and followed the scent trail to the street. He stopped at the end of the driveway to make sure Theo and Xander were still with him. Moving his head and nose back and forth, Yogi advanced down the street to the house past Xander's and stopped. He looked confused and sat down right there in the street.

"What is it, Yogi? What do you have?" Theo asked.

"Nothing," Yogi answered. "Nothing. The trail stops right here where I am sitting."

"That's not possible. It can't just stop."

"I'm not stupid," Yogi said, immediately regretting his

tone. "I am sorry, but it just stops right here," he softened.

THEO WILL FIND US

THE GATORS-BE-GONE VAN slowed to a stop.

"Where are we?" Julius whispered, poking his head out from under the canvas for a better look. "It looks like the middle of nowhere."

"Nowhere," Copycat agreed.

"I don't like this, Copycat. We're going to need to run and I mean fast. Follow me."

Parked at Ma's house, on the patch of dirt and gravel that served as a front yard. Elvis and Carl got out of their van, Fern close behind. The conversation had been easy, mostly revolving around what Ma might have cooked them for dinner. Chicken fried steak, it was unanimously decided, would hit the spot. With baked beans. Maybe some potato salad. Sweet tea. Fern had never eaten so well in her life. She heard a noise and turned.

"What the heck is that?"

Elvis and Carl turned together to see Julius and Copycat bolt from the back of their trailer and into the trees and scrub.

"Was that a coyote?"

"Looked like it."

"Was that a cat?"

"Looked like it."

"What the Hell?"

Fern knew. She was fully connected to the way of animals after having spent so much time with Pretty, Delroy, and Nika. In the wetlands. In the wild. That was no dog. That was a coyote and a cat. Period. But the boys were hungry and when the boys were hungry, not much else mattered. They all shrugged and went inside to smell the glorious smells coming out of the kitchen.

Julius and Copycat ran like the wind. Through thick brush, weaving through trees, and splashing through areas of shallow water. "Run, Copycat, run!"

"Run."

They did just that. They ran like felons from a crime scene. And they ran some more, not knowing where they were or where they were going. They only knew that these humans, with their trailer that smelled of dead things, hadn't been vetted by Theo.

After a long and chaotic dash through alien territory, Julius slowed then stopped. He was tiring and Copycat looked absolutely beat. "It's getting dark, Copycat." He lifted his nose. "And I smell things, creatures, that I have never smelled before." He scanned his surroundings. "I've got a bad feeling about this place. We will need to find some sort of shelter that I can defend. Hop on my back, Copycat. I can carry you. Hop on."

"Hop on," Copycat barely managed.

The two wayward souls eventually found a fallen tree on a dry patch of land. A refuge for the night. "It will be okay, Copycat. Theo will find us."

"Find us."

LOST CAT POSTERS

THE WHOLE CREW was in attendance. All of them. Agnes, distraught, drew some comfort from the gathering. Xander was there with Yogi, Theo, and Geppetto, along with Ripley, Figaro, and Digby.

"We will find them. We will," Theo tried to be encouraging. "Nobody has seen anything, heard anything, or knows anything. There must be something we are missing. So, we need to gather our thoughts and get organized."

"Yes, organize!" Ripley concurred.

"Organize and mobilize!" Digby added.

"Mobilize!" Figaro fairly shouted.

Theo was in charge. "Geppetto, fly over to that vulture you have been consorting with, find out if she has seen anything, knows anything. Maybe put together some sort of aerial search party." Theo paused to catch his breath. "Ripley, Fig, Dig, talk to Dante and see what he can do to help. Xander, let's you and I walk the streets with Yogi. It's almost dark, but Yogi has a good nose. We have to try."

Agnes didn't look too hopeful. "They are gone, Theo."

She started to cry once again.

Theo and Xander scoured the neighborhood with Yogi. "I don't know what else to do," was Theo's lament.

Xander didn't know what to do either. "Let's keep patrolling around the area. You know they may have just wandered off, sniffing and chasing after something."

"Julius wouldn't let Copycat wander off. He's too careful, too protective."

"I don't know, Theo. They might be back at Agnes's right now getting a scolding."

"I doubt it."

The two men had arrived back at the spot where Yogi had lost the scent. Yogi sat down once again. "The trail stops here. It simply stops. It doesn't make any sense," Yogi was looking at Theo as he spoke.

"You are right, Yogi. It makes no sense at all."

As Theo and Xander, Yogi along with them, neared a return to Agnes's house, they could see a flashlight in the dark, wobbling this way and that.

"Agnes. What are you doing?" Theo wanted to know.

"Here. Look at these." Agnes handed a sheet of paper to Theo and another to Xander. "I just printed about fifty of them on my computer."

Agnes had a handful of "Lost Cat" posters with her, complete with a black and white photo of Copycat, and was preparing to tape one to every light pole and every stop sign she could find. "Can't hurt."

"You're right, Agnes. It can't hurt. I will come with you, and we can do this together until your posters are gone." Or, until you run out of tape, was Xander's afterthought.

"Okay. You two be careful. I'm going back to see if there

is any news from the others," Theo said, with little hope. Something was seriously amiss. "We can restart the search party in the morning."

IS THE BIG BAD REAL?

FERN SAID GOODBYE to Diesel and Pretty as she got ready to leave for the day. "I'm going to go to work now with the boys. You two behave." She scratched Diesel under the chin and gave the giant iguana a pat on its bony head.

Elvis and Soop had the van loaded and ready to go. Fern, grunting, lifted the lunch cooler into the van. It was heavy with leftover chicken, sandwiched with sliced cheese and onion, and tomatoes. Lots of water, some Mountain Dew, and Oreos for dessert. Nice.

"Where are we going today?" Fern wanted to know.

"Same place. Somebody else called the homeowner's association about an alligator sighting, so we might as well check it out." Carl mused for a moment. "That place is super good business for us."

Partway through the thirty-minute drive, a thought popped into Fern's head. "Is The Big Bad real? Is he really out there somewhere?" She wondered aloud.

The boys were silent for a solid beat or two before Elvis

decided he would handle this. "It's a bit like kids and fairy tales, Fern. Sometimes what is real, and what we want to *believe* is real, are two different things. Sometimes they are the same." Elvis rubbed the stubble on his chin. Thinking. "Look at you, Fern. You talk to dogs and lizards and birds and whatever. It's hard to believe, but I've seen it with my own two eyes and heard it with my own two ears. So, it's difficult to say. What is real?"

Fern was considering this when Carl decided to chime in. "Sometimes it is a situation when you have to consider what is real and what you *fear* to be real."

This was a lot for Fern. Her head was spinning when she asked, "Do you fear The Big Bad?"

"No," Carl said. I remember, back in..." Carl caught himself in time. He almost said, Louisiana. But he didn't. Barely. "...back in the day, there was a gator the size of this van we're sitting in. We tracked him for a while, and I ain't afraid to tell you I was nervous as hell. But we got him. He was our "Big Bad" at the time. So, now we're not afraid of nothing."

"It was scary at the time," Elvis agreed.

A silence settled in between them, three souls considering the conversation and its true meaning.

"So, is The Big Bad real or not?" Fern wanted closure.

Elvis pulled the van over to the side of the road and stopped. He looked at Carl, Carl looked at him.

"Fern," Elvis began, "Fear is a motivator. Nothing brings people together more so than a common enemy. A common fear. It helps us forget whatever bad things that we might fear are lurking inside of us all. If we all can share a purpose, then that's what makes a community. In some other places, The Big Bad might be something completely different. Around here, it's a monster alligator, and if he's real, we'll catch him."

"Besides," added Carl, with a grin, "it's super good for business." After a moment's reflection, he added, "Make no mistake, Fern. Once we get him, there will be another Big Bad to take his place. There's always going to be a Big Bad."

Back on the road, Elvis thought about *bad*. His mind flashed back to Ma putting bullet holes into his Pa. Sometimes *bad* can be *good*.

AN EPIPHANY

EARLY MORNING, WITH the arsonist sun not yet torching the Floridians below, Karl was planning to investigate another tract of vacant land. This time in Titusville, a short drive north of Cocoa. He would first detour on his usual drive-by through Riverside Estates. It was necessary to fuel his hatred for Theo and Agnes, and he thrived on that hatred.

On his slow meander about the neighborhood, he noticed an awful lot of paper sheets taped to various light poles and road signs. What is all this crap? Before reaching Agnes's house he pulled his car over to inspect one of the posted sheets. He couldn't believe what he was looking at. He put the paper down and immediately snatched it back up to look again. A missing cat? Agnes's cat had gone missing. This was too good to be true. It had to be Agnes's cat. At the bottom of the paper were Agnes's name, address, and phone number. And the offer of a reward for information leading to a safe return. Fred. What a stupid name for a cat. The cheap old lady was a millionaire, thanks to Bobnoggin, and she was offering a lousy five hundred dollars for a reward? Karl snickered to himself.

The car ride to Titusville was an enjoyable one to be sure. Karl delighted in entertaining thoughts of "Fred" being eaten by a gator. Then he had an epiphany. What if...

THAT CAN'T BE GOOD

THE ELVIS AND Soop gator-catching van was brought to a stop in Riverside Estates and parked in front of an easement between a pair of houses that led to the intercoastal waterway. Elvis and Soop, followed by Fern, got out and each looked up to the sky, simultaneously coming to the same conclusion. It was going to be a hot one.

"I'll be back in a second," Fern said as she quick-walked to a light pole. What are all these papers she'd been noticing? She took down a sheet to check it out.

Beneath a photo of a cat, it read: "MISSING! Missing cat. He is a slightly overweight ginger and is probably scared. His name is Fred, but he sometimes responds to Copycat. PLEASE HELP! He might be in the company of a one-eyed dog who looks like a coyote but isn't. He's a dog. His name is Julius, and he is very protective, so be careful." It went on to detail a phone number and address and notice of reward. Fern sighed. As if some cretin would want a reward for returning a missing cat.

Fern dropped her hands, still clinging to the paper. She

looked at the address of the nearest house and quickly determined that the Agnes Tilray on the poster was just a few houses away from where she stood. From where they were parked yesterday. Fern knew immediately what had happened.

"Elvis! Soop!" Fern ran up to the brothers. "Look at this," she said, handing them the paper.

The boys looked at it together and then at Fern.

"That's the cat that jumped out the back of our trailer yesterday when we got home," Fern said, looking for agreement.

"I believe you are right," Carl said.

"Yup. That's them," Elvis was nodding his head. "The cat and the coyote. They ran off into the swamp and that can't be good."

"I'm going to go tell this lady we saw her cat." Fern made to leave.

"Hang on a second, Fern," Carl said. "That cat and the dog, or coyote, or whatever, took off into the swamp. You are just going to upset this woman. That cat isn't coming back and nobody's going to find it. It's gone and probably dead."

Elvis nodded his head. "You will just upset the lady."

Fern's brow darkened. "Who says nobody's going to find it?"

I HAVE FRIENDS

"OKAY, EVERYBODY. THERE'S no sign of Copycat or Julius. We have no choice but to continue to look around the neighborhood and hope somebody has seen them." Theo tried to sound encouraging.

The group had gathered that morning on the patio, not knowing what to do.

"Hello? Hello?" It was Fern coming into the backyard waving a poster in her hand. "Hi. I think I might be able to help."

All eyes were on the teenage-looking girl. Who's this? Haven't we seen her around here before? One of those gator catcher people?

"Hi," Fern repeated herself. "I think I saw your cat. And your coyote."

"Dog," Figaro corrected, drawing a look from Ripley *and* Fern who understood the correction and gave Figaro a knowing eye.

"Yesterday when we got home, we saw a cat and a coyote jump off the back of our trailer. They took off, south

I think, when they saw us. They looked scared."

Theo, Xander, Agnes, and the rest just glared at the girl.

Fern surmised aloud, "I think they jumped onto our trailer when we were parked here and, sort of, accidentally went for a ride when we left."

"Where is your home?" Agnes demanded.

"About a half hour west of here and a little south."

"There is nothing there but wetlands and brush," Xander said.

"That's right," came a man's voice. Elvis and Carl had entered the backyard to see what the heck Fern was up to. "There is nothing there," Elvis continued. "I'm real sorry, but that cat and coyote are in the thick of it now. I hate to tell you, but I'm not sure you're gonna see them again."

"I'm super sorry about it," Carl said with genuine empathy.

Elvis and Carl, along with Fern, introduced themselves to the group, expressing their concerns and understanding. Theo and Xander thanked them for their kind words, Agnes disconsolate, did not speak.

"I can understand her," Digby whispered. "The girl."

"Me too," Figaro whispered back. "But not those guys. I can understand her but not the men."

"Me too," Yogi concurred.

"You guys just shut up for a minute," Ripley warned.

"I'll tell you what, when I get home tonight, I will ask around. Maybe somebody has seen something." Fern tried to sound hopeful. "You never know."

"Ask around with whom?" Xander inquired in disbelief.

Fern considered her words. "I have friends." Pause. "I'll let you know."

* * *

Elvis, Carl, and Fern left the yard and trudged back to the van.

"I can't work," Fern said. "My heart's just not in it."

"Alright, me neither," Elvis agreed.

Carl pursed his lips and nodded. "The Big Bad can wait another day."

Putting their gear back in the van, none of them noticed a big black BMW do a slow pass, then speed away.

A LUCRATIVE PROPOSITION

KARL SNELL HAD hatched a plan on the drive home from a wasted afternoon in Titusville. It would give him meaning. It would bring him joy.

Back at his condo in Orlando, he poured two fingers of single malt whiskey and propped his feet on his coffee table. With an unsuppressed grin, he sipped his drink and dialed the number he had seen painted on the side of the Gators-Be-Gone van.

"Hello?" Elvis didn't recognize the number.

"Hi, my name is Karl Snell and I have a business proposition for you."

"Oh, yeah? Who is this?"

"A lucrative proposition. I was hoping we could meet to discuss this?"

"Meet? Who the hell is this?" Curious now: "How lucrative are we talking?" Elvis's suspicion dial was at eleven.

"Very." Karl began to wonder how much this might cost him. "I got your number off the side of your van. I've seen you working recently in Riverside Estates, and I am sure you have seen the missing cat posters all over the place."

"Yeah."

"Yeah, well, I want that cat."

"The side of our van says Gators-Be-Gone, not Cats-Be-Gone."

"If you don't want the job, just say so," Karl bluffed. "But I want that cat."

"How bad?"

"Bad."

Elvis waved his hands at Carl and then pointed a finger at his phone. You wouldn't believe this guy. "So, what now?"

"I'd like to meet. You tell me when and where."

"I don't know. Gimme a sec." Elvis tapped *mute* on his phone. "Soop, this might be interesting. Toni's tonight?"

Soop nodded. Out for a beer? Why not?

"Meet us at Toni's off King Street. West of Cocoa. Seven o'clock."

"What's Toni's?"

"A bar."

"I'll be there."

Elvis told Carl what was what, and told Carl not to tell Fern, not yet. Let's first see what this idiot wants.

JUST GOT OFF A PLANE

KARL HAD THE rest of the afternoon to figure out what he was going to wear to Toni's. A roadside bar, he decided, would be full of locals and not so many tourists. He needed to look the part, so he stopped at a couple of places to assess the sartorial preferences of the local huckleberries.

At Peeper's Bar and Grill, a silly name, he thought, he ordered a craft beer. He couldn't help himself. Looking around, he played a game in his head. Who is local, who isn't. Apparently, a lot of tourists liked to hang out at Peeper's and pretend to be local. Cargo shorts: Tourist. Sensible walking shoes: Tourist. Gaudy floral shirt: Tourist. Oversized sunglasses that fit over your prescription glasses: Tourist. A flaming red, sunburned face: Tourist. A walking, talking melanoma incubator from *up north*. The locals, he concluded, were wearing jeans and t-shirts. Maybe a western shirt. Maybe boots.

He spied a tall and lanky guy with dusty jeans and boots, a Tractor Supply cap on backward, a Lynyrd Skynyrd hairdo, and single-digit body fat. The ladies seemed to love him for whatever reason. I could never pull that off.

After checking in on a few other roadside drinking establishments, Karl decided on the look he was after. He knew he didn't want to look like he just got off a plane from *up north*, so he went shopping. At a Boot Barn, he was talked into a pair of square-toe stockman boots. How much? Are you kidding me? At Target, he got a pair of Wrangler jeans and a t-shirt to wear under his new snap-front western shirt. He drew the line at wearing a hat.

He went back to his condo to try on his new duds and then to google-map Toni's. He didn't want to be late. This is going to be interesting. I hope.

THEY NEEDED HOPE

"EVERYBODY, THIS IS Nancy. Nancy, this is everybody. My friends." Geppetto surveyed the gathering. "Nancy and I are going to be the eyes in the sky. We will assist in the search in any way that we can."

There was an appreciative murmuring amongst the squirrels, then: "Hello, Nancy. I'm Figaro."

"Hello, Figaro."

Fig took a beat and then asked, "So, I don't wish to seem forward, but what happened to your face?"

"What?"

"Your face. You don't have any feathers on your face."

"FIGARO!" It was Ripley.

"That's okay," Nancy said. "I am a turkey vulture. A red vulture. We don't, any of us, have any feathers on our heads."

"Why not?" Figaro couldn't quite process this.

"Because we eat dead meat. We are carrion eaters. There is a lot of blood and guts at dinner time, so we have evolved to have no feathers to get all clogged up with, well, blood and guts when we eat. It gets pretty messy

114

sometimes."

"Oh." Makes sense, Fig thought. Not really, maybe sort of. Kind of gross, but fine.

Agnes was despondent. She could barely drag herself around. Fred. Poor Fred. Theo was at the patio table, as were Xander and Yogi. They all had trouble mustering the energy to do anything. What could they do to find Julius and Copycat? Wander around in the swamp? They needed direction. They needed a lead. They needed hope.

SHE OWES YOU

ELVIS AND CARL told Fern they were going out for a drink. A guy thing, but they would be back soon enough. Fern was left to chit-chat with Ma for a bit, before going outside to hang with Diesel and Pretty.

"I saw Delroy earlier this afternoon," Pretty said. She was a little embarrassed that she forgot to mention it to Fern before now.

"What? Delroy?"

"Yes, Delroy."

Delroy was just what Fern needed. A five-hundred-foot view over the swamp. "If you see him again, I want to talk to him." She was firm in her tone.

"Well, there he is right there." Pretty was looking up. "Right there, just flying around trying to sniff out some dead meat for his dinner."

Fern jumped to her feet and started waving frantically at the sky, hoping Delroy would see her. Of course, he did. The big black vulture executed a few lazy circles on his way down to meet Fern. Diesel was in the prone position, head resting on his paws, completely disinterested. He had already met the bird.

"Delroy!" Fern almost started clapping her hands in delight. "Where have you been? Why don't you visit more often? It is so good to see you."

"Hi, Fern. You look well."

You look well? That's it? Fern hid her disappointment, expecting a more enthusiastic greeting from the vulture. "Delroy, what have you been doing? Is anybody looking for me back in Tampa?"

"Not that I can tell. All seems good." Delroy cocked his head. "I've learned that you made friends with that Panther. Well played, Fern. I'm not sure how you did it. By the way, the big cat seems to have recovered from her injury."

"That's good news. I'm happy for her." Pause. "How do you know this?"

"I spoke to Nika, just a few days ago. From a safe distance, of course. She says she owes you."

Fern was pacing. Thinking.

"What's the matter, Fern? You seem agitated." The vulture was curious.

"I need you to help me."

"Okay, sure."

"I want to do a favor for an older lady that I just met. Her cat is missing."

"Yeah?"

"The cat's name is Fred. Maybe Copycat. I'm not quite sure. There is a coyote with him, and the two of them are lost out there somewhere." Fern waved her hands. "Out there."

"In the swamp? There is a cat and a coyote wandering around out there in the swamp?"

"Yes."

"So, what do you want me to do?"

"See if you can find them."

"It's going to be dark soon, but, yeah, I'll take a quick look. Give me an hour, or so. Don't expect much, but I will try."

"I love you, Delroy!"

YOU SPELL IT WRONG

ELVIS AND CARL sat at the bar, drinking domestic beer. Not that fruity stuff that the tourists wanted. Notes of citrus? No. PBR and Bud. Thanks.

"You expecting someone?" asked Toni from behind the bar.

"Yeah. Not sure about this, but whatever," Elvis said.

"I think a guy from *up north*. Wants to talk business," was Carl's contribution.

"This might be him." Toni was looking toward the door.

In walked Karl, resplendent in his new clothes. He looked around, pretending he belonged. He didn't. This was a *nest* of hard men, drinking after a hard day. The bar smelled of sweat and spilled beer. He spotted Elvis and Carl at the bar. That's them.

"Hi, I'm Karl Snell." He held out his hand, first to Elvis.

"Elvis," was the noncommittal reply. He shook Karl's hand and immediately thought: Wuss from *up north*.

"Hi," Karl said turning to Carl. "How're you doing?"

"Super good. So, what's your name again?"

"Karl. Karl with a "K.""

"Oh." He considered this for a beat. "So, you spell it wrong." Carl fake-smiled.

Drinks were ordered and Karl was introduced to Toni. A Farrah Fawcett look-alike. Wow, thought Karl. Hot. At least in a seventies sort of way. "So, you own the place?" His look was lecherous, although he figured he was just being friendly.

"Name's on the sign." Toni snarked as she turned to get the drinks.

"Karl, you are off to a bad start. Seriously. She already don't like you. Don't screw with Toni. Really." Carl shook his head. Who is this guy?

"What do you want to talk to us about?" Elvis was getting down to business.

"Well, Agnes Tilray is an old friend. I have known her a long time, and it happens I owe her a favor. I'd like to repay that favor."

"What kind of favor?"

"A big one. She is a lovely woman. and I don't want her to suffer the pain of losing her beloved cat."

Carl looked at him askance. "So, what do you expect us to do?"

"Find her cat."

"How're we supposed to do that?" Elvis wanted to know.

"I see your truck around here all the time. All around Riverside Estates. You are professional, um, catchers of wildlife. Or so it seems. That cat has got to be around there somewhere. If you should somehow find her cat, bring it to me. Not her. I want to be the hero. I want to give her back her cat. That way I can repay the favor."

"And, what's that worth to you?" Carl was digging. He didn't want to tell this knucklehead that the cat wasn't lost in Riverside Estates, it was lost in the swamp.

"A lot."

"How much?"

"A lot."

"How much is a lot?"

Karl knew this was the make-or-break moment. But he fancied himself as a master negotiator. He had been doing this for a lifetime. "One thousand dollars."

Elvis and Carl burst out laughing.

"Two thousand dollars." Karl upped the ante.

The brothers kept laughing and laughing.

"You ain't here to give some old lady her cat for two thousand dollars." Elvis smiled. "You are here because you want that stank-ass cat for your own no-good reasons."

Karl grinned. Game on. "Five thousand."

Elvis and Carl exchanged glances. Now we are talking.

"Let us think on it," Elvis said. "We might have ourselves a deal."

A STATE OF FLUX

JULIUS WOULD HAVE liked to have awakened with the dawn. He didn't. Not at dawn that is. He had been up most of the night. The symphony of the swamp prevented any sleep. Crickets chirping, frogs croaking, boars grunting. Strange noises from strange creatures.

"Let's go, Copycat. We need to keep moving."

"Keep moving."

"I don't know where it is we're going, but it's someplace not here."

"Not here."

Julius and Copycat were in a state of flux, suffocating from their indecision. This way? That way? Who knew? They had to keep moving, or a bear, or panther, or something else, would find them and make them a meal.

Copycat was at a ragged edge. The two vagabonds would surely succumb to the swamp if Theo didn't find them soon.

Water was a necessity. Food was a necessity. What would they do?

* * *

"What's that?" Julius said aloud. "What's that sound?"

A wild boar burst through a thicket, grunting and posturing. My territory. The beast fake-charged at Julius, all bravado and not much finesse. It stopped abruptly, flashing its cartoonishly-large tusks.

"What do you want?" Julius demanded.

"You."

"You can't have me."

"I will have what I want." The boar charged again at Julius.

Julius dodged. "Copycat, you got my back? Got it?"

"Got it," Copycat replied, ready for battle.

The coyote deked and danced until the boar grew tired. "You will not have me, pig."

"I will," said the boar. "I will have you when you are least prepared. You will wait for me and I will not come. And you will wait and wait, and I still will not come. When exhaustion overtakes you, then I will come."

"I will be ready."

"Ready," confirmed the ginger cat. His energy renewed. Ready to back his friend.

EVERYBODY HAS A GUN

THEO AND THE crew had gathered once again. Picking at their breakfast pancakes, disconsolate. Nobody with a plan worth anything. Then Fern showed up in the backyard and everybody stared.

"Don't ask how," Fern began, "but I know that your cat and your dog might be west of here. Not far, but in the thick of things and they are alive. At least they were last night."

"How do you know this?" Xander asked already knowing the answer.

"I said don't ask. I have friends."

What kind of friends would know this? Theo and the rest wondered in silence.

"If you are going to go looking, I would take 519 south through Rockledge and then any old dirt road you can find going west." Fern assessed the two men. "I wouldn't advise it, but I know what it is to love an animal. It will be dangerous, so you need to be prepared for just about anything. Good luck."

Fern turned to leave and caught Figaro's eye. "Hi there."

"Hi," Figaro replied.

Theo stared. He felt as if in a twilight zone. She is *talking* to Figaro.

Xander wanted to take charge, so, Theo let him, sort of. The animals were grouped around, waiting for instruction.

"Theo. Please tell the squirrels to stay put in case our two friends somehow wander home." Xander paused for a moment. "However unlikely that might be."

Theo took over. "Rip, Fig, Dig. Stay here. Listen and watch for information that we might have missed. Anything. Talk to Dante. Yogi, stay with the squirrels and use that smeller of yours. Geppetto and Nancy, aerial surveillance, please. Look west of here, toward where the sun sets. Xander and I are going on a rescue mission." Theo looked each squirrel in the eye. "To the swamp."

Theo exhaled and looked over at the tall Afghan. "Are you going to be okay with this?"

Xander wondered whom Theo thought he was talking to.

Xander ran back to his house with Yogi. He jammed some items in a backpack: Fly spray, some protein bars, a flashlight, and some bottled water. A few minutes later he reappeared, strapped and ready. He had his Walther PDP 9mm carry gun inside his belt and had his Colt Python . 357 Magnum revolver holstered on his hip. He was set.

"You got a gun, Theo?" Xander inquired.

"Uh, no. Why would I have a gun?"

"I just thought..."

"I do!" Agnes said.

"What?"

"I do. I have one."

"What?"

"Hang on, Nogs, my dear." Agnes ran away into the house and then reappeared with a Smith & Wesson M&P 15 assault rifle. The magazine was loaded with 5.56 NATO rounds. Thirty of them.

"Here you go my darling," she said, handing Theo the craziest-looking gun he had ever seen.

"Where the hell did you get this?" Theo wanted to know. Wide-eyed.

"The store."

"What are you doing with a gun?"

"It's Florida. Everybody has a gun." Agnes wondered what the big deal was. "It was on sale."

Theo shook his head, exasperated. "I wouldn't know how to even use this thing.

"I got it, Theo," Xander interjected. "Give it to me. I am familiar with this type of weapon."

Theo looked at Xander and wondered what world he was living in. "Okay. I guess."

"Agnes?" Xander looked at the rifle and back at Agnes. "This has been modified."

"Yes, I know. It goes full auto. I paid extra in cash."

"Who did you pay?"

"The guy at the store. He wanted cash." Agnes shrugged. No big deal.

"Here, take my Walther," Xander offered. "It's a good gun," he said, handing it to Theo. "Full mag, nothing chambered, so if you need to fire it, you'll have to rack your slide."

Theo nodded even though he wasn't sure what all that meant.

A SNAKE WITH A LOT OF MONEY

"YOU'RE TOO YOUNG to be drinking beer," Elvis declared with very little conviction.

"You're right," Fern laughed. "I only want one."

"He's right, you're too young." Carl was a half beat behind.

They were sitting in fold-up lawn chairs around the fire pit. Diesel was bored and snoozing. Pretty was sitting tight at Fern's side.

"Let me tell you something," slurred Elvis. "There's things we talk about and things we don't talk about. This is going to be one of those things."

Carl just about died laughing. "Which one of those things? The ones we talk about or the ones we don't?"

"The ones that…" Elvis was confused. "The one of those things. You know. Those things."

Carl was laughing so hard, he could hardly stand it.

Fern was amused but impatient. She had a plan. This plan of hers was one of those things you *don't* talk about.

"We met this fella last night at the bar. He's from *up*

north. Or, he used to be, I guess," Elvis mused.

"He don't even spell his own name right!" Carl was still laughing his head off.

"He *doesn't* spell his name properly." Fern was correcting Carl's grammar.

"That's right! His name is Carl too, but he spells it with a K!" This produced a gale of laughter from both Carl and Elvis.

Fern got up to fetch another round of beer from the cooler. These boys will be passed out and in bed soon. She hoped.

"So, the thing is, Fern, this Karl-with-a-K guy? He's a snake. He's bad news. He came into Toni's with brand new boots and jeans trying to act local." Elvis looked at Fern to make sure she was paying attention.

"But that ain't what makes him a snake," Carl added. "He's a snake with a lot of money. How do I know this you might ask? Because that fool offered us five thousand dollars to find that missing cat. Can you believe that?"

"Five thousand for a cat!" Elvis said as if it was the most preposterous thing in the world.

"You can't do that!" Fern yelled at the men. "That cat belongs to Agnes Tilray!"

Elvis was taken aback. "He says he's going to give it to her. He wants to be the hero."

"Do you believe him? You just said he was a snake." Fern, slightly calmer now. Slightly.

"No, I don't believe him," Carl confirmed. "He's a snake with a lot of money, but you can't trust a guy who can't even spell his own name right."

"Well, that cat is probably a goner by now, anyway," Elvis opined." So, let's just not talk about it. I don't want anyone to go and tell Agnes and get her upset. She seems nice."

Fern picked up the empty cans around the fire pit and tossed them into the recycle container. The men had brushed their teeth and had whispered a goodnight to Ma who was already asleep.

Fern found some paper and a pen in the kitchen where she scribbled a note for the Pettigrews. They wouldn't see it until morning and Fern would be long gone by then. She filled her trusty backpack with some leftovers from the fridge and some bottled water. Pretty knew what Fern was going to do but said nothing. On the way out the front door, Fern spied Ma's .22 rifle and thought it might be a good idea to *borrow* it. "Let's go, Pretty," she whispered.

Fern shook her head and put a finger to her lips in a silent *sshhh* to Diesel and left the backyard, heading into the wetlands. "Don't worry, Pretty. Delroy will be keeping an eye on us. It'll be fine."

GET MOVING

MA WAS FUMING. No breakfast for the boys today. Only coffee.

"You boys get in here, now. Sit down and don't talk. I'm doing the talking."

"Where's Fern?" Carl foolishly inquired.

Ma lowered her voice to a rasping growl. When Ma was annoyed, she would raise her voice, but when full-on angry, she growled. "I said," staring at Carl, "I'm doing the talking." Ma gathered herself. She was holding the note that Fern had left on the kitchen table. "Fern is gone. She left last night after you two numbskulls went to bed. She says she's gone to look for that old lady's cat. She is out there in the swamp someplace. She took Pretty with her, and she took my .22, so at least she has that."

Elvis and Carl gave each other an *uh oh* look. They were in the deep end now.

Ma gave her two boys a moment to consider the trouble they were in. "I trusted you to look after Fern. She's just a kid. So, now you boys are going to find her. Do not even think about coming back without her in one piece. Do you understand me?" Ma glared at them with feral intensity. "Now get moving."

Elvis and Carl worked together like practiced dance partners. Each knew what to do. Get the flat bottom boat out of the shed and an extra gas can with it. Fly spray. Food, water, Mountain Dew. Binoculars. A first aid kit, just in case. Carl had his trusty knife, but they needed guns with extra ammo. Elvis had a Mossberg 12-gauge pump shotgun and a 9mm Glock 19 sidearm. Carl had his Winchester rifle chambered in .30-30 rounds. They were taking things very seriously.

"Let's go, Diesel. You're coming with us. We need your nose."

Elvis and Carl dragged the boat to the estuary at the end of the yard and pushed it into the water. Carl started the small outboard motor bolted on the back of the boat, then they both risked a look back at the house. They didn't like what they saw. Ma on the front porch with her hands on her hips and death-rays shooting from her eyes.

CHECK YOUR FEET

THEO AND XANDER took the Audi. If Julius and Copycat see it, or smell the smells in it, they would come. They drove, as advised, south to Rockledge, and then turning west past I-95 they found what looked like an old dirt road that might lead to a boat launch or a hunting camp. When the road stopped, they found neither. The road just stopped for no discernible reason.

"This is where we get out," Theo said, realizing there was no other option. "Let's grab our gear."

And our guns, Xander thought to himself.

They each downed a bottle of water so they wouldn't have to carry the weight in their packs, and set off. The two men followed some sort of trail into the wetlands, trying to navigate from one patch of dry land to the next. They met with little success and were soaked to the knees in no time. This wasn't going to be easy.

Theo checked his phone. He had a vehicle locater app that would light up a thin red line on a map that would lead them back to the Audi. He didn't want to get lost out here in the middle of nowhere.

"Check your feet, Theo," Xander said. "Always watch where you are walking. You don't want to step on a rattlesnake."

Theo was surprised. "Rattlesnake? They have rattlesnakes here?" He had thought they were only in the dusty southwest for some reason. Maybe from watching cowboy movies as a kid. Tumbleweeds and rattlesnakes.

"They do. Lots of them. Eastern diamondback rattlesnakes. If you step on one, you will wish you hadn't," Xander was walking in front, he had point, and turned to catch Theo's eyes. "That's why we are going home before it gets dark. Cat or no cat, coyote or no coyote. We can always try again tomorrow."

"Every day that goes by, things will look a little grimmer for them. We have flashlights, we can stay past dark even if only for a short while."

"No chance, Theo. Not happening. Not in the dark."

The men trudged along in silence for some time, not really knowing what they were doing. Were Copycat and Julius going to suddenly appear on the trail in front of them? No.

"Do you have snakes in Afghanistan, Xander?"

"Yes, and some of them deadly to be sure."

"What kind?" Theo was making conversation to ease his nervousness.

"We have cobras and vipers and kraits. There are others, but these are the worst. Especially the kraits. Afghans know to be careful, but I have seen Western soldiers bitten. I know of an infantryman from Wisconsin who pulled on his boots without checking first. A krait was inside and bit him on the foot. It was an ugly thing to see, and that soldier never made it home."

They traipsed along for what seemed like forever. Theo was thinking that a machete would have been nice. In a small clearing, he checked a cerulean sky to see if he could spot Geppetto and Nancy. No luck. If they had to come back tomorrow, he would ask the two birds to stay close by and in regular contact.

DO YOU HAVE A MACHETE?

THEO PULLED HIS SUV into Agnes's driveway where he and Xander got out. Ripley and her two kids were up in a tree and knew immediately from the deflated posture of the two men that they had not found Copycat and Julius. Their friends were still missing.

Agnes came out the front door, took one glance at Theo and Xander, then turned and went back inside. She was starting to come apart. She went to her bedroom and didn't come out for an hour. She knew she needed to hold it together, but it was hard. Nevertheless, she thought, the men were trying, and she needed to support them. I'll get them some food.

Theo and Xander were seated at the patio table when Agnes appeared carrying a tray of ham and cheese sandwiches with the crusts cut off. She thought that would make it look like she had made an effort to make them seem fancy. And somehow tastier. The two men couldn't have been more grateful.

"No wine?" Theo was half joking. Only half.

"I'll be right back."

"We tried, Agnes," Theo began. "We really did. But, in the end, we were just wandering around. I figure if Julius was anywhere close by, he would have smelled us."

"We will go back in the morning," Xander promised.

"I know you will," Agnes smiled a smile of sadness.

The three of them continued their muted conversation, each trying desperately to sound upbeat and encouraging. The trio of squirrels, along with Yogi, were listening in, understanding only Theo, and trying to parse together the gist of their conversation.

"Agnes?" It was Theo.

"Yes?"

"Do you have a machete?"

"Why would I have a machete?"

"I don't know, you have a freaking machine gun. So I kind of figured that a machete wouldn't be entirely unreasonable."

Theo went to bed and dreamed of snakes. Bad snakes.

THE HUMANS ALL HAD GUNS

THEO AND XANDER were looking for Copycat and Julius. Fern and Pretty were doing the same. Elvis and Carl were looking for Fern. Copycat and Julius were looking for a way home.

Everybody was in the swamp, all of them looking for someone or something. And all were discouraged.

The wildlife had teeth and claws and fangs and tusks. They had extraordinary olfactory senses and superior night vision. They could swim and climb and move with Darwinian stealth. They also had home territory knowledge.

The humans all had guns.

The edge goes to the wildlife. Maybe.

Elvis and Carl had grown up in the swamp, had been seasoned on the bayou, and knew the wetlands like no other human could.

Fern was a Seminole of the Wind Clan and *believed* that gave her (true or not) special advantage. She felt at home in the wilderness with her friend, Pretty. Besides, she could talk to animals.

Xander was a veteran of a horrible war, a crack shot, and always composed. Even in dire circumstances.

Theo had the unique strength of an absolutely unyielding resolve. Besides, he also could talk to animals.

A WARM HUG

FERN WAS BLEARY-EYED from lack of sleep. "C'mon Pretty, let's keep going."

Pretty had eaten a full share of crickets and was snoozing in a state of postprandial somnolence. Sleeping with one eye open, as iguanas are wont to do, she cracked wide the other and glared at Fern.

"Pretty! Let's go. Help me keep an eye out for Delroy."

Pretty climbed down from the tree branch that had served as her resting place and joined Fern in the middle of a small clearing. She looked up. "I don't see Delroy, but I'm wondering about these two birds."

Fern was also looking skyward. A large red turkey vulture and a black crow were flying together in wide circles. "That looks odd."

"Odd isn't the word. Flat-out strange is more like it." Pretty was trying to process what she was looking at. "A vulture and a crow? Flying together? I have never seen that before."

Fern hoisted her backpack over one shoulder, picked up her rifle, and froze. Pretty was dead still beside her. Both of them stared, frozen in absolute silence.

A large and sleek panther had appeared from nowhere and was standing, motionless, about ten yards away. It was Nika.

"Hello, Fern. Have you come to hunt me with that gun?" Nika lowered her head and moved one paw forward. Then another, slowly waving her black-tipped tail.

"Nika? Is that you?"

"It is."

"I haven't come to hunt you, Nika." Fern slowly placed her rifle on the ground. "I've come to hug you!" She spread her arms wide and then with some trepidation, moved toward the big cat.

Nika allowed it. A warm hug from a human. She rubbed her whiskered head against Fern's and purred like a chainsaw.

Pretty was resigned to the fact that there would be no end to the strangeness of the swamp.

"How is your paw, Nika? Here, let me see." Fern held out her hand as if saying "paw" to a golden retriever in exchange for a treat.

Nika complied without a second thought.

"It looks good. Any pain?"

"No, none."

"That's good to hear."

"Why are you out here Fern? This is a dangerous place to be wandering around." Nika was curious.

"Well, now that you mention it, maybe you could help us?"

IT'S A GAME TRAIL

THEO AND XANDER stopped at a landscaping and garden center on their way through Rockledge. It would be another rescue mission this day and they weren't going back to the swamp without a machete. Theo had insisted. Purchase made, the two men went back to the same place they had parked the day before, at the end of the dirt road. They chose what looked to be a different trail leading into the wetlands and re-started the search.

An hour in, Theo stopped. "Xander?"

"Yeah?"

"This half-ass trail we are following?"

"Yeah?"

"What is it? Who made this trail?"

Xander thought for a moment. How do I explain this? "It's a game trail, Theo." What else would it be?

"What kind of game?"

"Wild hogs probably. Pigs."

"That's great. All we need is some deranged boar with three-inch tusks charging through here."

"Don't worry, Theo," Xander laughed. "You could

always talk to it and make friends!"

"Sure. If given the chance, I suppose I would try."

"Or I could shoot it for you," Xander laughed again.

They continued their trek. "Theo, do you remember our conversation the other night? I told you about the boy in Afghanistan who would talk to the goats? I said that you and he were not the only ones, and there may well be more?"

Theo knew where this was going. "You want to talk about the girl. The one who came into our backyard. You know what, Xander? I was thinking the same thing."

"She has the same gift, Theo. It was plain to see. When she told us she would ask around about Copycat and Julius, she mentioned her friends. I believe she meant *animal* friends."

"I believe you are right," Theo conceded. "When this is all over, I'm going to have a long talk with her. She needs to know she is not alone."

"I believe she already knows."

WATER IS DANGEROUS

JULIUS AND COPYCAT continued their unfortunate journey through the wetlands. What's that sound? A woodpecker? They should have known. Even the familiar was strange to them now as their nerves were shot. Anxiety and doubt were festering within them both. Julius could smell *so many* smells and none of them were of the familiar woodlands back at home. His working assumption was that everything was dangerous. Every smell would portend a threat.

The one-eyed coyote stopped in a small clearing. "Copycat, we need some sort of plan."

"Plan."

Julius thought for a moment. "Do you think that big hog is around here somewhere?"

Copycat scanned the surroundings. "Somewhere."

"Well, if that one isn't around, then another one is. And, probably just as rude."

Julius sighed in his coyote way of sighing and looked up.

The sky had thought to rain that day, spat briefly upon

the world below, and then changed its mind, bringing clouds and relentlessly oppressive heat.

Copycat walked in circles as if losing his grasp on reality.

Julius pointed his snout upward. "Look up there, Copycat. Do you see that black vulture?"

No response from the ginger.

"Think about it. You know Theo is looking for us, right? And we both know he will bring Geppetto for help. So, maybe if we stay put in one place, eventually Geppetto will fly over and bring Theo to save us." He paused for a beat to see if the cat was listening. "It might not be the greatest plan ever, but it's all I have. We need to keep believing in Theo."

Copycat continued walking in circles, muttering, "Theo, Theo," over and over again.

Julius was growing concerned with Copycat's mental state. The cat had no Theo, no Agnes, and no Figaro. No ice cream and no cozy bed - just this unending heat and thirst. Copycat needed food and water, but around here, water is dangerous.

COME AND FIND ME

DELROY HAD FLOWN down from up high to join Fern and Pretty, who were still talking to Nika.

"Everybody has a job to do. Delroy, you do your thing and bring me intel when you have it," Fern advised the big black vulture.

"I have some now," Delroy began.

"What is it?"

"There is a crow and a turkey vulture flying around together. They must be looking for the same thing we are."

"I've seen them," Fern confirmed. "I think they must be on Theo's team. If you see them again, maybe you could share intelligence with them."

"Got it."

"Nika? You are the most gifted tracker anywhere. Use your skills. Look for the cat and the coyote, but be careful. From what I can gather, that coyote is protective and experienced."

"Do I look worried?" Nika scoffed, in the way only an apex predator can.

"Pretty, you stay with me." Fern looked each in the eye.

"Everybody good? Any news, come and find me."

I'LL PAY EXTRA

KARL WAS ANXIOUS for some news. He didn't want to bother Elvis and Carl in case they would think him too anxious and jack up the price. But he had to know. He needed to be in the loop. He had driven through Riverside Estates and did not see the Gators-Be-Gone van anywhere. Aren't they supposed to be looking for that damn cat?

Standing on the flat-bottomed boat, vigilant, Elvis felt his phone vibrate in his jeans pocket. He looked at it and turned to Carl. "Hey, Soop, it's your buddy. Karl with a K."

Carl rolled his eyes and shut off the outboard motor. "What does that imbecile want?"

"Let's find out," Elvis said while he thumbed his phone. "Hello?"

"Hello, it's Karl Snell."

"Yeah, Karl with a K. What's up?"

"I'm just checking in. How is it going with the search for poor Mrs. Tilray's cat?"

"It's going. Still working on it."

What is this crap? Working on it? They are probably drinking at Toni's. "Well, I drove through Riverside Estates today and I didn't see you guys. So, I was wondering what was what?"

"Karl," Elvis began. "I do have some news. That cat ain't chasing skinks around Riverside Estates. That cat is out in the swamp somewhere, running around with some coyote."

"What? The swamp?" Karl was confused. "The swamp?"

"Yeah, the swamp. We're looking. Looking hard."

"How do you know this, Elvis? That cat got lost at Riverside Estates. I saw the posters."

"I know this 'cause I saw that cat and that coyote jump off our truck and run off, straight into the swamp. That's how I know." Elvis was growing annoyed. "Me and Soop are out here looking right now. You want us to keep looking?"

"Yes! Yes! Keep looking. I want that cat."

"Well, it's going to cost you extra now." Elvis glanced over at Carl who appreciated the *cost extra* part. "We're out in the swamp, not some tidy old-folks community."

"That's okay. I'll pay extra. Just get that cat. Can you do that?"

"Can do Mr. Snell. We'll find him." And then: "How much extra are we talking?" Elvis winked at Carl.

Elvis disconnected. "He says six thousand."

"That guy is nuts," Carl said. "But right now, the most important thing is finding Fern. Not that cat."

Elvis agreed, thinking about Ma. Worried about Ma.

THE HEADLESS SNAKE

THEO AND XANDER continued along their way, trudging through the swamp and brush, but happy to have the machete to make things easier. The boredom from the slog was making them irritable. The conversation had slowed to a monosyllabic grunt here and there, in between complaints about the heat and humidity. They were soaked to their knees and were being eaten alive by insects.

"Hold up, Xander." Theo wanted to stop in a clearing, a small patch of dry land.

"What now?" Xander wanted to know. Hot, sweaty, and impatient.

"Calm down. I just need some water and a short break." Theo took a can of fly spray from his backpack.

Before Theo could take the cap off the spray can, Xander said, "Don't move." His voice low and intense.

Theo looked at the tall Afghan and felt his blood run cold. Xander had his Colt Python drawn and in a two-handed grip. What is this? Theo could not finish processing the thought. Xander lowered the barrel of his revolver to point at Theo's feet.

"Do. Not. Move."

The sound of the single round being fired was as loud as anything Theo had ever heard. He looked down, half expecting to see his feet blown to bits. He saw, instead, the body of a sizable snake, writhing and twisting, turning itself into knots. Its head was gone. Obliterated. Only the body remained and was in its death throes.

"That used to be an eastern diamondback rattlesnake," Xander deadpanned. "Not anymore."

Theo was transfixed at the dead, but still writhing, body of the headless snake. Shaken, he eventually looked up at Xander and thanked him.

"Don't worry about it. It's not the first snake I ever shot."

After regaining some measure of composure, Theo took point as they continued their seemingly futile mission. Not the first *snake* he ever shot? What else has he shot? Theo feared he already knew the answer.

A SERIOUS GUN

GEPPETTO AND NANCY heard the gunshot and wheeled down to a treetop to talk.

"We need to check in on Theo and Xander," Geppetto said, with a measure of concern.

"Agreed," Nancy acknowledged. "Like, now."

Delroy heard the shot and immediately altered his flight path. He had been executing a grid pattern but became nervous at the sound of a gun. Find Fern and Pretty.

Nika heard the shot and flinched. She stopped and smelled the air. Not good. A gun meant humans. And humans hunt. With guns.

Fern heard the shot and looked at Pretty. Yeah, I heard that too.

Elvis and Carl had shut down their small outboard motor and were making their way through shallow water, pushing along the bottom with long poles. Diesel was content, just sniffing the air. *So many* interesting smells in the swamp.

"Woah!" Elvis stopped poling. "Hear that?"

"Yeah, I heard that." Carl was estimating the distance. Sound. Weapon caliber. Considering the echoes through the trees. Processing limited information.

"That was a big gun," Elvis concluded.

"A serious gun," Carl said, nodding. "It weren't no .22 - not Fern."

"A single shot. He's good. Only one shot."

"That wasn't no tourist shooting at some pigs for a selfie to put on the 'gram."

"Nope."

"One shot. One kill."

"Yup. He's good."

Julius and Copycat just looked at each other. A gunshot. What does that mean?

SOON I THINK

REENA WAS LOUNGING on the outrageously expensive sofa in Gerda's newly assumed condo, fiddling with her phone, yawning. She was a leopard in a tree branch. Bored but content.

"Would you like a glass of wine?" Gerda inquired from the kitchen.

"Sure."

"Red or white?"

"Whatever you're having."

Gerda extracted a bottle of white from the wine fridge. A 2005 Puligny-Montrachet. It was a Grand Cru and egregiously priced. She poured a glass for herself and brought another over to Reena. "What are you doing?"

Reena looked up from her phone. "Wordle. I'm stuck."

"Let me see," Gerda offered.

Reena showed her the phone and said, "I have the "a" and the "g" but can't figure out the rest."

Gerda looked at the phone, scanned the remaining and available letters, and knew the answer immediately, but didn't want Reena to feel stupid. She hemmed and hawed, pretending to not know the answer. "I don't know, Reena. Try 'augur'."

Reena tapped in the letters. "You are right! Well done!" Reena had already figured out the answer but wanted to give Gerda the opportunity to come up with it on her own. It was the game they played. Neither of them sincere, both of them pretending. Each sometimes wondering about the other.

Reena put her phone down and sipped her wine. Delicious. "When are we going to do this thing, Gerda?"

"My father will call when it is time."

"Do you always do exactly what your father tells you? And when?"

"Look around, Reena."

Reena did.

"As long as my father is paying for all of this, then yes."

Reena considered Gerda's response. It was certainly a nice life. So, when Daddy says jump, you jump and don't ask questions. She understood.

"It will be soon, Reena. I'm just waiting for the call. In the meantime, we should do a scouting mission."

"What kind of scouting mission?

"We are looking for cameras. We already know the animal clinic doesn't have them installed yet, and Bobnoggin doesn't have any, but we need to cruise down Sycamore Lane and check everybody else. I need access and I don't want to be on someone's doorbell cam."

"Okay, that makes sense," Reena agreed. "What about cops? Don't they have cameras on street poles, or at intersections?"

"Not here in Ashburn. It's not exactly a crime-ridden town."

"ALPR systems? Automatic license plate readers?"

Reena pushed the point.

"They might have them on police cruisers, but that's about it."

Gerda handed Reena a pair of binoculars. "You spy while I drive."

ADVANTAGE KARL

GERDA WAS AT the wheel of her Benz, Reena next to her in the passenger seat, both enjoying the drive.

"How far?" Reena asked.

"Ten minutes," Gerda replied, just as the infotainment screen on her dashboard lit up. The caller ID said "Loser" so she kept the call on the car speakers. She wanted Reena to hear the conversation, if only to prove to her what an idiot her brother was.

"What?"

"Hello, Gerda."

"What do you want, Karl?"

"I just wanted you to know that whatever you are working on up there, it's nothing compared to what I have cooking in my oven."

"Oh, really? What could you possibly have *cooking* that would be more important than what I am doing?"

Karl paused for a moment, thinking this would enhance the importance of what he was about to say. "I'm going to have Agnes Tilray's cat kidnapped."

Gerda turned to Reena and gave her a look. I told you

this guy was a moron. Reena tried not to laugh.

"Karl, have you been drinking? A cat? This is your big plan for revenge?"

"Listen to me, darling sister. The cat is already missing. It ran off into the swamp with Bobnoggin's coyote. I am going to find that cat before Bobnoggin does. He is out there thinking he's Crocodile Dundee, looking for that cat. He wants to be the hero. But he won't."

"Karl, I'm not joking. I have very real concerns about your mental health. How are you going to find that cat in the middle of a swamp? And so what if you do?"

"Well, it so happens I have hired some professionals to find that cat for me. I'm going to pay them a handsome sum. They're real pros."

"Professional cat-catchers? Karl, you've lost it." Gerda turned into a grocery store parking lot. She couldn't concentrate on driving and have this inane conversation at the same time. Reena giggled and shrugged. "So, this is your revenge? A cat?" Gerda intoned her words more as a statement than a question.

"Sister of mine, I need Bobnoggin to fail. I need Agnes Tilray to be crushed. It will bring me joy."

"What will you do with the cat if they catch it for you?"

"Kill it and send it to her."

Gerda slowly shook her head. "You are a victim of your emotions, Karl. I don't care about any of that. I just want to do business. You want to address some inner inadequacy, whereas I want to make money."

"And how will you do that?"

"I'm going to burn his house down! And that stupid animal clinic with it. I will burn them to the ground and there will be nothing left but a heap of ashes."

Karl could not quite believe what he was hearing. Burn

down Bobnoggin's house? And the clinic? He knew he would get it out of her sooner or later, but he had not expected her to just blurt it out. Not something involving such extreme measures. "Don't you think that's a bit much, Gerda? I mean, really. How will this make you money? Where is the payoff?"

"You want people crushed? This will crush both of them. Bobnoggin *and* the old lady. This will be your revenge, Karl. After his house and that clinic are gone, maybe he will just move to Florida with his pets and live out his days down there."

"Again, where is the payoff?"

"I will be able to re-open talks with Paul Gentry at the Ashburn Golf and Country Club. I get the land and flip it to the club so they can put in their tennis courts, Karl. That's the payoff. It is what you should have done last year, but you didn't have the stomach for it. You are forever too busy slipping on the banana peels of life."

"When will you be doing this?"

Click.

Karl had known his sister would eventually tell him what she was up to, but this was a bridge too far. The worst he would do is kill a cat, so what? Sure, he would lie, cheat, steal, and murder animals, whatever. But arson was a completely different story. That takes things to a whole new level. He shook his head and smiled.

After Gerda composed herself, she left the parking lot and headed toward Sycamore Lane. "Okay, Reena, get your binoculars out. We are looking for doorbell cameras."

They cruised the neighborhood and saw very little of anything. A few homes had a doorbell camera, but there were so many trees lining the long driveways, those cameras would have limited range. A restricted field of vision. At best, they might record someone on the front porch, and that's about it.

On the drive home, not much was said. Gerda was still bothered by her idiot brother and his plan to kidnap a cat. Moron. He would never be the real deal. He was not psychologically equipped.

Reena sat in silence, looking out the window and thinking. Maybe Karl wasn't so stupid after all. He might be an asshole, but he's a clever asshole. Gerda had just been goaded into giving Karl information about a major crime they were going to commit. A serious felony. She had gifted him knowledge and knowledge was power. Advantage Karl.

"Does Karl know about me?" Reena was more than a little curious. She needed to know.

"Why would I discuss my personal life with him?" Gerda didn't understand where this question was coming from.

"Just asking."

A PANTHER NEARBY

AFTER MACHETEING HIS way through some brush, the game trail randomly disappearing and reappearing, Theo glanced back at Xander. The Afghan never appeared tired or thirsty. He's a machine, Theo marveled to himself. "I'm going to need some water, Xander."

"That's fine. Let's stop here for a quick break," Xander said, looking around the small clearing.

Theo, having learned his lesson, was very careful to look around his feet as he stepped.

Geppetto landed first, followed closely by Nancy. "Are you okay?" the crow said, looking directly at Theo. "We heard a gunshot."

"We're fine," Theo reassured his friend, happy to see him. "Xander, I believe, might have saved my life."

"How? What happened?"

"I almost stepped on a rattlesnake. Xander killed it. Shot its head off."

Geppetto nodded his beak, as did Nancy, while appraising Xander. This guy is the real deal.

"Well, if we heard that shot, so did everybody and everything around here. Julius and Copycat will be scared and might go into hiding. We have been flying around and haven't seen much, but you should know there is a panther prowling around, so be careful," Geppetto cautioned.

"A panther?" Theo said, drawing a raised-eyebrow look from Xander.

"Have you seen it? How close?" Great. First wild hogs and now a panther.

"No, I haven't seen it, but I have a reliable source," Geppetto replied. "A black vulture named Delroy told me," he continued, as if that would make perfect sense to Theo.

"We also saw two men floating around in a boat," Nancy volunteered. "They seem to be looking for something, or someone."

"Thank you, Nancy." Theo was grateful for the information.

"We are going to take off and see what we can see," Geppetto advised, then added, "If you two are going to keep searching, don't go that way." He beak-pointed.

Xander gazed in wonderment, understanding only what Theo was saying as his friend continued his chit-chat with the birds. "What are they saying?"

"They say they haven't seen much of anything except there is a panther nearby and there are two men in a boat searching for something. It might be Elvis and Soop."

Xander nodded his head, now worried about the panther.

"They also said we shouldn't go that way," Theo continued, pointing his chin.

"Why not?" Xander wondered.

"Why not that way?" Theo addressed Geppetto.

"There is a group of pigs over there and one of them is a large black boar with some fearsome-looking tusks. If he is the pugnacious sort, you would probably have to shoot him."

Theo turned to Xander after the crow was finished speaking. "Geppetto says there are a bunch of wild hogs over there." Message received.

NOT TODAY, LIZARD

JULIUS AND COPYCAT forged ahead through the wetlands and brush, looking for a suitable place to stay put. They were hoping to be spotted by Geppetto or even found by Theo. Occasionally they would come to areas where they would need to cross water, making them both exceptionally skittish. On land, they could run, or even fight if, necessary, but the water was not home turf and they had heard all about the alligators infesting the swamp. They were also aware of the rumors about The Big Bad.

"Copycat, we need to cross."

"Cross."

Julius stared at the water in front of him. It was quiet. Disconcertingly quiet. It wasn't far, but he was unsure of its depth. "I think we will need to swim," he said.

"Swim."

The Big Bad could first *feel* the presence of fools before he could smell them. He was lounging, submerged, ten feet from the shoreline. He smelled then heard a coyote and a small cat. What would they be doing together? He waited. Were they ignorant enough to try to cross?

Something held Julius back. "I don't know Copycat. I sense danger." The coyote lifted his nose, seeking information and finding none.

Copycat could see that Julius was nervous, which made *him* nervous as well.

"We should not cross here, Copycat. I don't like this place. We can look for a different spot."

The Big Bad had had enough. He lifted his massive head just enough for his eyes to clear the waterline. Are they leaving? Not yet. The Big Bad swooshed his tail and launched. His huge black body heaved out of the water, jaws wide and seeking purchase on the coyote in front of him.

Julius and Copycat were startled; the electricity of a sudden jolt of adrenaline coursed through them. Copycat executed a four-paw jump straight into the air, stumbling as he landed, before righting himself. Julius spun, the front of his body quicker than his rear. The Big Bad gnashed at a hind leg, grasping and severing a paw before losing his grip.

I've missed, thought the brute. Wait, he's bleeding. I will take him now. The coyote is down. Half of his leathery body still in the water and half on land, The Big Bad prepared for another attack, when he himself was attacked.

Copycat was not unfamiliar with battle. He had once fought Julius before they became friends. He had once faced the legendary coyote-with-no-name in defense of Julius. Something synthesized within him, and he left himself. An otherworldly rage consuming him, Copycat screamed a scream that gave even The Big Bad pause. Claws out and teeth bared, the ginger house cat who would be less than a snack for the giant gator, streaked over Julius and landed on The Big Bad's head. He was going for the eyes. He wanted to blind the monster.

With a toss of his head, The Big Bad sent Copycat flying and saw him land in the clearing away from the water.

Julius was up but knew he was badly injured. "Run! Copycat, run!" The coyote turned to face his enemy. He couldn't run, but he would fight. He would buy Copycat some time.

The Big Bad opened his mouth in a low growl and leaped at Julius, this time gaining a solid hold on the coyote's rear quarters, tearing at both of his hind legs. Ripping off bits of bone and flesh, he retreated a few feet to watch and to enjoy the pain of the dog's death.

Copycat sped to Julius. Standing over his friend's still-alive body, he gave the gator a death glare.

"How quaint," the alligator said, the sarcasm dripping from its mouth. "I suppose I will have to kill you too."

"Go, Copycat. Run while you can. Leave me." Julius was prone, bleeding profusely, and gasping his dying breaths.

Copycat stared. *This cat doesn't run. This cat fights. This cat will not leave you, Julius.*

Panthers do not roar. They growl and they snarl. For a panther to issue a low growl is to issue a warning. A high-pitched snarl is to signal imminent savagery. A supernatural sound tore through the swamp, unlike anything the swamp had ever heard, and it *stilled* nature. It was a sound to freeze blood in its veins; a sound born of fury.

The Big Bad stopped and stared as Nika burst through a thicket and landed at the water's edge.

"Not today, lizard." Her ears were pinned and saliva dripped from her teeth.

The Big Bad slid backward, into a comfortable depth. Not today, he agreed, wisdom triumphing over imprudence.

"Copycat, Nika said. "We must leave. That gator's not going anywhere for long. It's not safe."

Copycat looked up at the enormous cat.

"My name is Nika. I can take you to a safe place. To good people who will take you home."

"Home?"

Julius was supine, bleeding copiously, and yet oddly comfortable. The tenuous light of his life was still in his eyes, but growing dim. "I love you, Copycat."

The light went out.

Copycat was unable to respond. Unable to move.

"We have to leave," Nika said. "I will take you to Fern. You will like her, she can talk. You will understand her."

Copycat still would not leave. He would not leave Julius.

"We have to go," Nika insisted. "You cannot fight that thing. Your vengeance will be hollow. It always is. Julius would not want you dissolving in the acid inside that monster's stomach."

Copycat *still* would not leave.

Nika, in the way of maternalistic cats, bent to grab Copycat in her teeth, by his scruff, and carried him away.

COVERED IN BLOOD

GEPPETTO AND NANCY were circling at five hundred feet in a tranquil sky when Nancy said, "I smell something."

"What?"

"Blood."

They found Julius's dead body on the grass near the water. Crows don't cry. Geppetto wanted to, but was unable. His old nemesis and now dear friend had been killed. He didn't know what to do. His next thought was of Copycat who was nowhere to be seen.

"Where is the cat?" Nancy wondered aloud.

Geppetto snapped to alert. "I don't know, but I have to find Theo. Like, now. You stay here and keep any creatures away from Julius. Don't you dare even peck at him."

"I wouldn't eat a friend." Nancy cocked her head to one side. "Or even the friend of a friend."

Geppetto found Theo and Xander, indefatigable on their quixotic mission, trampling through the swamp.

"Geppetto, do you have any news?" Theo knew the crow would not have arrived without something to say.

"I do." Geppetto hadn't the words, nor the courage to tell Theo. Better for him to see for himself. "Follow me. I will fly in a straight line and make stops so you can keep up. Just follow me."

Theo and Xander followed the crow; quick, double-time. Xander knew in his heart that this would not be good. Theo knew also, and his breathing became labored.

They came into the clearing where Julius's body was lying, Nancy standing watch as promised.

The Big Bad was also watching. Amused.

Theo dropped his pack and his machete and threw himself on top of the dead coyote, holding his head in his arms. Theo's mouth worked up and down, but no sound came out save a high-pitched keening. He was agonized and saliva began to dribble from his mouth. He had nursed his *dog* to health after more than one scrape, and numerous injuries. He had brought new life to Julius, with the help of Doc Nicky, and had made him the unofficial captain of the team back at the sanctuary in Illinois. Julius was a fixture. Loved and respected by all, best friend to Figaro and greatest friend to Copycat.

Xander had seen his share and more of grieving and knew when to step back. Space was needed. It was necessary at times like this.

Biologically incapable of crying, Geppetto began to slam his face into the side of a tree. He needed to feel something.

He wanted to feel Theo's pain. Nancy stopped him and rubbed her beak against his.

Theo stood. He was covered in blood and had retribution in his eyes. He was barely able to speak between short, truncated breaths. "This was an alligator."

Xander agreed. "A very big and bad alligator."

Theo swiveled his head back and forth. Frantic now. "Copycat?' Then, at the top of his lungs, he screamed, "COPYCAT!" Nature was once again stilled.

Geppetto had regained some measure of composure. "I don't know where he is, Theo. He is not here and that means he has escaped. Somehow."

"I will look for him," Nancy said.

"I will fly with you."

"We will find him, Theo." Xander wanted to reassure his friend. "But we must go now. If Copycat is okay, he will be nearby." And then added, "I'm sure he's okay."

The men left Julius behind, Theo swearing he would come back to bury him. Copycat was their primary concern now. Slogging through the brush and wetlands yet again, Theo stopped and declared: "You go. You find Copycat. I'll catch up to you, but there is something I need to do first."

Xander didn't like the sound of this at all. "What are you going to do?"

"You go. Find Copycat. I will be back. I'll get to you." With that, Theo reversed course, back toward Julius and The Big Bad.

DO YOUR JOB

MARCY DINGLE SHOWED Karl into his father's office. With a smirk and an eye-roll, she closed the door behind her.

"Sit down, Karl." Herman was looking out his office window like an obsessive, watching the planes fly in and out of Orlando International Airport.

Karl sat. He wasn't wearing a necktie this time but was, nevertheless, resplendent in a sublime Armani suit.

Herman eased into his chair and sighed in exasperation. "I've seen your report, Karl, and all you are bringing me are suggestions for developing vacant lots. Why is that?"

"I.."

"Vacant lots? Why can't you bring me something in a *good* location? If there is something at a good location, we can buy it and tear it down. The best locations will have something already there. Find something good and we can *negotiate* with the owners. I want land we can flip to the Cubans for their chicken joints. Not a patch of dirt. Why can't you understand this?"

"I..."

"Never mind. Just do your job for once." Herman stood and paced behind his desk. "Something else," he began before sitting back down. He had a pained expression. "I want you to go out tomorrow night. Make a reservation at Lonny's and get a nice steak dinner. Hang out at the bar and buy people drinks. Leave a big tip. Put it all on your credit card and then expense it."

"But…"

"Because I want you to be seen, and I want a paper trail. So, shut up and just do it."

Karl smirked to himself on the way down in the elevator. It's on. Gerda's grand plan will go down tomorrow night.

I'VE BEEN WAITING FOR YOU

JULIUS WAS WARM and comfortable. He seemed to be floating in the air, looking down on Copycat. He saw his friend walking with a large panther and somehow Julius knew Copycat was safe. They traveled through some trees and then entered a clearing where a young woman and a big green iguana were waiting for them. His brave and precious companion, his brother in arms, was going to be okay.

There was a light pulling Julius *up*, higher into the sky. It was a soft white light, and he knew it to be inescapable, and that he would travel to that light. But he wasn't ready to go just yet. He had friends to whom he wanted to wish a quiet goodbye.

Julius floated, suspended, until, with his one good eye he could see Agnes sitting on her back patio table. Rip, Fig, and Dig were there with her. Figaro was eating nuts from a bowl. His much-adored friend looked up, and in that moment Julius thought that Figaro might see him. But the most heroic and fearless red squirrel who had ever lived, went back to his nuts. Goodbye, Figaro. I could not have loved you more.

The soft light still pulled, but Julius was not yet ready to let go. In a blink, he was over the Theodore Bobnoggin Animal Sanctuary back in Illinois. There was the animal clinic that was Theo's pride. He could see Doc Nicky in front of the clinic waving and smiling at Cierra and Riley as they walked hand-in-hand toward their car in the parking lot. The tall girl that Theo so loved, and her handsome boyfriend.

In Theo's backyard, there was Oscar the skunk sleeping in some shade, and Buster the rabbit chewing on some greenery. Buster seemed to have made some new rabbit friends as there were too many to count.

Hendrix, the owl who had taken his eye, was there, in a tree. He watched Hendrix take flight as if there were something amiss. How do owls know these things? Julius watched some more. He could see his boys, Marcus and Evander, prowling the golf course behind Theo's backyard. Hendrix was circling behind the animal clinic. There was an intruder. Julius spotted the coyote-with-no-name. His mortal enemy, the coyote who had taken his mate, Cleo. The coyote who had rendered his boys motherless. The coyote he had faced down and vanquished. The coyote Theo had almost shot dead with Agnes's gun. He was back. But with the comfort and surety of the afterlife, Julius knew Marcus and Evander would protect the sanctuary. He knew also, that Hendrix could deliver death from above in defense of the allied territory. His word was his bond. All would be well.

Julius was magically transported back over the swamp where he saw Theo. The man who had welcomed him into the backyard alliance. The man who brought him in and loved him, a predator with one eye scarred shut. The man who had nursed him back to health and had cared for him like family. Theodore Bobnoggin, the gentleman who had never before raised his voice, was below Julius now. He was drenched in blood and holding a gun in one hand and a machete in the other. There was no doubting what he would do. Theo was red-soaked, arms wide, and his face pointing skyward. There was a sound coming from him that was not human. It was a full-on, raging and screeching. Over and over again, Theo filled his lungs and let loose his anguish, his body shaking. Theo was a beast going to war.

Julius knew in his soul that Theo would have his vengeance. Theo was going to fight The Big Bad. He was going to unleash his wrath on the alligator. Theo was going to kill The Big Bad and Julius knew this with the certainty of a God, as no God would take Theo from the world. Goodbye, Theo. The world needs you.

The soft white light would not wait any longer. It pulled Julius skyward, carefully and gently. Julius could see an opening at the end of this tunnel of light when he heard a voice. The voice of his mate, the mother of his boys.

"Julius, my love."

"Cleo?"

"Welcome to heaven. I've been waiting for you."

THE BEAST IS ENORMOUS

FERN AND PRETTY were resting on a patch of dry land, unsure of their direction. The gunshot had them apprehensive about their own safety.

"Maybe we should wait here for Nika or Delroy to bring us some information?"

"Information?" Pretty questioned. "It was a gun that we heard. That means humans, so unless it was Elvis or Soop, we might be in some trouble."

"I have a gun too," Fern reminded Pretty. "But I think we might be best served waiting here to see what might develop."

"Or, to see who or what might show up."

Delroy showed up.

Fern ate the last of the crusty sandwich that she had pilfered from Ma's fridge. Pretty wandered around, like some prehistoric thing transported in time through a wormhole to the present day.

"What's that?" Fern thought she heard something.

* * *

Nika came through the brush and proudly deposited Copycat, unhurt, on the ground in front of Fern. "I believe this might be the cat you have been looking for?"

"I believe you are right! I think. Are you Copycat?" Fern was in disbelief.

"Copycat."

Nika purred, nuzzling Copycat. "This is a long story. And a sad one." Nika gave Pretty a nod, hello. "I found him doing battle with The Big Bad. I can give you details later, but it was horrible. You can't imagine." Nika paused an appropriate pause before continuing. "The coyote didn't make it. Julius died defending Copycat and Copycat was almost killed defending Julius. Copycat is worthy of any panther's respect. It was something to see."

"Oh, no, I am so sorry Copycat that you lost your friend," Fern said gently, trying to console the cat.

"Friend," Copycat said. *The big cat was right. This girl can talk just like Theo.*

Fern, back to Nika: "What happened to The Big Bad?"

"He lives. He slithered back into the water when I challenged him, and I am glad he did. The beast is enormous."

"I don't know how to thank you, Nika. You are remarkable," beamed Fern.

"Remarkable," Copycat agreed.

"Come here," Fern sat and stretched her arms to receive the ginger. "Come and let me hug you."

Copycat complied and curled up on Fern's lap. He hadn't known how badly he needed a warm hug.

"I'm so incredibly sorry about your friend. He sounds like a friend worth having."

Pretty was watching this. "I would hug him too, but I

don't know how that might work."

THUNDER

AFTER LEAVING THE scene of Julius's final battle, Geppetto and Nancy took flight in search of Copycat. They would stay ahead of Theo and Xander and then fly back with news. Good or bad.

Geppetto did not get far. He was despairing at the death of his friend. He took roost in a high tree and was immediately joined by Nancy.

"Geppetto, I know this is hard for you, but we have to think about Copycat now."

The crow stared into space.

"I have seen my share of death. I am a vulture, remember? I see it daily. Dead animals who had family and friends. Now gone. I am not oblivious to this; I am not uncaring."

Geppetto was unmoved. He had lost Julius and he hadn't been there to help him.

Nancy was losing patience. "Listen to me, crow. We have a job to do. We must find Copycat. He is in danger, especially without Julius beside him. What would Julius think if the *puppet master* didn't fly to save Copycat? Julius is counting on you. So, fly. Fly with me and I will fly with you, my friend. Together we will find Copycat."

Geppetto came to his senses. Nancy was right. With a growing respect for the red turkey vulture who had called him friend, he took to the air. Nancy with him, at his side. Which, of course, is what friends do.

It wasn't long before they were joined by a black vulture. "I know what you are looking for."

The three birds flew down to rest on a cypress tree.

"My name is Delroy. I am a friend of Fern and of Pretty. The ugly iguana. But don't tell her I said that."

"What news do you have?" It was Nancy.

"Your cat is safe. Safe and well. Fern has her."

Geppetto and Nancy exchanged glances.

"Follow me," Delroy encouraged.

So, they did.

In the clearing with Fern and Pretty was a svelte panther. Geppetto peeled off and Nancy followed. "Wait, wait. Copycat is there! I see him!"

Geppetto turned, mid-flight, to see the fat and lazy ginger, his friend, cuddled up on a young woman's lap. He folded his wings like a hawk and dived, landing in the clearing.

"Copycat!" Geppetto was eyeing the panther as he greeted his old friend. "Copycat, you're safe!"

"Safe." Copycat cuddled a little closer to Fern.

Nancy landed close to Geppetto. Delroy landed close to Fern. Nika just watched, amazed at the oddity spread before her. A black vulture, a red turkey vulture, a crow, an iguana, and a house cat. And a human talking to all of them. What is *wrong* with the swamp today?

Words and greetings were exchanged, proper introductions made, and summaries of events told.

In the end, it was sad and happy at the same time. Nobody knew quite how to feel.

Then they heard thunder. The cracking thunder of guns.

Geppetto and Nancy took flight. Find Theo.

IT WAS AN EXPLOSION

THEO MOVED WITH purpose along the game trail, back to where Julius was lying dead. As he got closer to the scene, Theo's breathing became ragged. He was not of mind. He was out of control. He began heaving his lungs and as he got closer to the water and Julius's body, he began to scream. It was an unearthly noise that erupted from his mouth, spittle flying. He had Xander's Walther 9mm pistol in one hand and his machete in the other. He was sobbing and screeching at the same time. His whole body shook. He was going to kill The Big Bad or The Big Bad was going to kill him. One or the other. It was time for Theo to slay his demon. He had failed his wife when covid-19 overtook her. He had begged and prayed to whatever God might listen, to no avail. There was nothing he could do and there was nobody for him to blame. This time would be different. Now he had a monster. He had a target. The Big Bad had taken Julius and Theo would exact his vengeance.

The Big Bad was watching and waiting. The imbecile human is screaming at the sky and stumbling closer to the water's edge. Why is he making it so easy for me? Why do

I understand what he is saying? He floated just under the surface, moving ever so slowly toward the bank. Who is this man covered in the blood of my kill? And *why* do I understand him? Questions to befuddle even The Big Bad.

"Come to me Big Bad. Come to meet your end!" Theo shrieked at the dark water. "Come to face me and I will make you into a pair of boots!"

The Big Bad raised his head above the water's surface. He had heard rumors of a Seminole girl talking to animals and had dismissed it as nonsense. Now he had a human talking to him? Disrespectfully? "What fool are you? You dare to challenge me?"

Theo dropped his machete and pointed his gun at the creature's head. "Come to face me!"

So, the gator did just that. He swished his tail and burst from the water, stopping short of Theo, and with its jaws wide, bellowed a ghastly warning to the human. "I assume you are here because of the coyote? That's my guess. I would say I am sorry, but I am not. I killed him and I enjoyed it."

"But why? Why did you kill him?"

"Because I had to."

"Why did you have to?"

"Because I am The Big Bad."

Theo racked the slide on his pistol and fired his weapon. He was shaking and keening as he pulled the trigger and he kept going until the magazine was empty. He had fired fifteen rounds and eleven had missed. But four had hit their mark, bloodying the head of the creature.

Xander froze in his tracks on the game trail. It was the sound of war. Xander knew that sound. Theo had confronted The Big Bad. Xander dropped his pack and adjusted his rifle on its sling. He had been trained by the best of the best in Afghanistan. He was a professional assassin and knew what to do. With absolute composure, he moved swiftly along the trail, toward the sound of gunfire, muzzle down but ready. He had to get to Theo.

"Yeah? Yeah?" Theo was unhinged. "Yeah?"

The Big Bad was hurt and knew it. But still alive and ready to fight. He swung his body and head to snap at Theo. He knocked the human off his feet, but no blood was drawn. He displayed his gaping mouth once again, bellowing and growling.

Theo dropped his empty gun and picked up his machete, ready for the denouement with the beast. "You are not The Big Bad. No. *I* am The Big Bad! I am *your* Big Bad!" Theo shrieked. Wielding his machete like a samurai warrior, Theodore Bobnoggin approached the wounded gator, half on land and half in the water. Saliva slobbering from his mouth, his poise long gone, Theo roared, "I am *your* Big bad!" With that, the gentleman from *up north* swung his machete downward, burying it sideways across the snout of the behemoth.

The alligator's pain was deafening. He gaped his mouth wide in a final booming fury and made a last-ditch lunge toward Theo.

Xander would not allow it. No. Not his friend. Not this extraordinary man he had come to know as *special*. Xander clicked to full auto, shouldered his weapon, and delivered thirty rounds of armor penetrating, full metal jacket, 5.56 NATO rounds from his assault rifle into the maw of the devil. It was an explosion of blood and guts.

FIND FERN

ELVIS STIFFENED, AS did Carl. That wasn't a gunshot. That was a war zone.

"Enough," Elvis said. "Let's get to shore. Diesel, we need you. We need to find Fern, like, NOW."

Carl steered the flat-bottomed boat to a place where they could pull the boat onto land and tie it off on a tree. They grabbed their packs and guns and looked around. This needs to happen in a hurry. They had come to love Fern like a sister. Besides, if they didn't find Fern, Ma would slice them up like a loaf of bread.

"Diesel, go. Hunt. Find Fern."

So, the dog did. With urgency. He didn't know the words, but fully understood the tone.

I HAVE INFORMATION

KARL WAS AT home, tired of driving around and looking at empty lots, or buildings they could buy and tear down. Some of them might actually be good prospects, but there was more on his mind. A plot needing to be fully hatched. A scheme fully schemed. He went through the pros and cons. Weighing the scenarios, best to worst. If this, then that.

He poured himself a scotch, gave it a full sniff, and put his feet up on his living room coffee table. Sans shoes. This plan is going to work. You can't just burn down a man's house. Not and get away with it. He picked up his cell phone.

"Law offices of Fischer and Basse, how may I help you?"
    "Bruno Fischer, please."
    "May I ask who is calling?"
    "Snell, Karl Snell."

"I have a Mr. Karl Snell on the line for you."
    "Karl Snell?"

"That's what he said."

Bruno Fischer palmed his face. Karl Snell. I thought he was gone? Pause. Long pause. "Put him through."

"Hello, Karl, I thought you were in Florida?"

"I am."

"Okay, so how can I help you?"

"I have information about a major felony that will be perpetrated tomorrow night."

Perpetrated? He thinks he's a lawyer? *Perpetrated?* It's a shame he is still a client. "What are you talking about, Karl?"

"Somebody is going to burn down Theodore Bobnoggin's house on Sycamore Lane."

"What?"

"Yeah, burn it down, and the animal clinic next door."

Oh, jeez. A two-fisted eye rub. Snell calling me with this. "What are you talking about, Karl? Arson? How do you know this and why are you telling me?"

"I can't tell you how I know. I only want to do the right thing, Bruno. I don't want this to happen."

"Hold on. I'll be right back." Bruno Fischer put the call on hold. He knew damn well there wasn't an altruistic bone in Karl's body. He took a big gulp of his coffee. What is he up to? "Okay, sorry. I'm back. So, what do you want me to do?"

"I want you to stop it from happening. I want you to call the police with a credible and anonymous source telling you that this is what's going down. Tomorrow night."

"I thought you hated Bobnoggin?"

"I do. But I am not a complete asshole."

"Karl, I'm not calling anyone unless I know this is bona

fide. How do you know this? Who is going to do this?"

"My sister."

"Your sister?"

"Yes. At the direction of my father."

Karl was delighted with himself. Who has slipped on the banana peel this time, sister?

COULD NOT MASK THE SORROW

XANDER GENTLY PUT his arms around Theo and hugged him in the way that men do. "He is dead. You have avenged Julius. Come here, my friend."

Theo was shuddering. "I killed him? I killed The Big Bad?"

"You did. You killed him." Xander knew that this would not be the end. It was never the end. "You have killed The Big Bad gator." Xander would explain to him later, not now, how the spirit of The Big Bad would never die. There is always a Big Bad.

"Theo, I will tell the story of *you,* for as long as I live. I will tell the story of your courage and your bravery in the face of the monster. But, for now, we must go."

Geppetto flew down, his wings fluttering to ease him to a gentle stop, landing in the clearing. "I heard guns, Theo. Are you okay?" Geppetto quickly realized that everything was not okay. "Theo? Theo? Are you all right?" The bird turned his head from Theo to Xander and back again, looking for clues.

"I'm fine, I'm fine." Theo had brought himself back under control, with a strength and resolve that few men possess. "Thank you, Xander, Thank you." Then at Geppetto: "Have you seen Copycat? Where is Nancy?"

"I have news, Theo. It is wonderful news. Our Copycat is safe!" The crow paused as if anticipating a thunderous ovation. He was met with silent stares. "Copycat is safe!" Geppetto repeated with a little more enthusiasm.

An understanding of what he had just heard, finally washed over Theo. "Copycat is safe. Found and safe," Theo whispered to himself in relief.

Xander was relieved for Agnes, Theo was relieved for Agnes and himself and everyone back in Illinois and most of all for Figaro. To explain to the little red squirrel with an immense heart that he had lost both Julius and Copycat at the same time - it would be unbearable for him.

"Safe? How is he safe?" Theo demanded snapping his attention back to the crow. "Where is he, Geppetto? Where is Copycat?"

"Wait and I will tell you. I can give you the headlines for now and the details later. I think you might want to head back to your car while you have the chance, you will barely make it before dark and, no offense, but Theo, you look like a hot mess. You need a shower and will probably just want to throw those clothes away."

"Forget my clothes, Geppetto, just tell me where Copycat is."

"You are going to find this hard to believe, but here goes," Geppetto started before being interrupted by Nancy landing in the clearing next to him.

"Is that a gator?" Nancy asked with an astonished look.

"Used to be," Geppetto observed.

"Where is his head?"

"From the looks of Theo, I would say he might have had something to do with it."

"Theo killed The Big Bad?" Nancy was trying to reel it all in.

"That appears to be the case."

"Geppetto!" Theo was growing impatient.

"Copycat is with Fern. The girl from the gator-catching company. She has been out here looking for Copycat this whole time. She is amazing. And guess what? She can actually talk to animals just like you!"

"Yes, I have come to learn just that. Where are they now? Fern and Copycat?"

"That way," Geppetto gestured with his head. "They are with a big green iguana and a black vulture and a very large panther."

"A panther?" Theo's heart jumped.

"A panther?" Xander repeated to his friend.

"Yes, a panther. It was the panther who saved Copycat from being eaten by The Big Bad. The panther is named *Nika,* and she is friends with Fern. I am going back there now to let them know you are okay. They got concerned with all that gunfire."

Nancy flew off to give Copycat and Fern the news that Theo and Xander were fine. Geppetto stayed behind for a couple of minutes.

"Are you telling me that Copycat was rescued by a panther and brought to a teenage girl who talks to animals?" Theo was shaking his head.

"Yes. And this girl seems to have a lot of friends. They will get back to Fern's house and probably bring Copycat to Agnes in the morning. You should get started before it gets too dark. I'm going to fly quickly to tell Copycat and the rest that you are safe, Nancy is telling them now, but Copycat will want to hear it from me. I will fly back to meet you."

Theo and Xander were both shaky and exhausted. The adrenaline rush had turned into an adrenaline crash. The euphoria of bloodlust, the slaughter of The Big Bad, and the joy of learning Copycat was alive and safe, could not mask the sorrow of having lost Julius. They were emotionally and physically spent and on the verge of collapse. It was only the urgency of telling Agnes the good news about Copycat that kept them going. So, they trudged. And trudged.

Thirty minutes later, Geppetto caught back up to them just as they reached the Audi.

"All is good, Theo. Copycat will be back home first thing in the morning. Now, let's go and tell Agnes."

"And Figaro," Theo managed a smile as he climbed into his SUV, along with Xander and the crow he had come to admire so much.

FINE WITH ME

GEPPETTO ARRIVED BACK at the small clearing where Fern, Copycat, and the rest were being regaled by Nancy.

"Oh, yes. It was quite a scene." Nancy pieced together the information she had and created a narrative to *thrill* for the ages. "Theo and the other man had shot The Big Bad full of holes, but the beast would not die. That was the gunfire we heard. Geppetto had flown ahead of me and dove down to peck at the monster's head, trying to blind it. The men had run out of ammunition, so Theo attacked the giant gator with his machete and then his bare hands. His bare hands!" Nancy scanned the clearing, enjoying the wide-eyed attention of her listeners before continuing her monumental embellishment and the aggrandizement of her beau, the crow. "I have never seen such bravery. Geppetto was fighting for his friend and Theo was a madman bent on revenge for Julius. Geppetto was thrown from the beast when I raced to him with great worry. I turned to see Theo grow in size and in strength to rip the gator's head from its body and throw it in the water. He then raised his face in victory and screamed at the sky. He had won. He had defeated The Big Bad. It was truly amazing. This man was utterly undaunted in his vengeance and then," Nancy had spied Geppetto's arrival at the edge of the grass, "the bravery of Geppetto to actually do combat with The Big Bad." Nancy acted as if she had just noticed Geppetto's presence. "Oh, hello, Geppetto."

Nika, always on alert, had slipped out of the clearing and circled back around. Downwind from the scent of dog and the scent of humans. Two humans and their dog. Hunting.

Diesel had picked up the scent of Fern and was waggy-tailed leading Elvis and Carl through some trees and brush. Elvis was right behind Diesel with his shotgun at the ready, Soop was right behind them both with his Winchester rifle. Too much gunfire lately and too much of it was close by. It put them both on edge.

Diesel stopped wagging his tail and sat down. He had the scent of Fern and Pretty, but he also had the scent of birds and *two* cats. One of the cats was big and not to be trifled with.

"This way, Diesel? Which way? Which way to Fern, Diesel? C'mon. Take me to Fern." It was Elvis encouraging his dog.

Everything happened all at once. The quietly happy group in the clearing was moments from leaving to get back to the Pettigrew house. All were discussing who was going with them and who was going their own way for now. Geppetto had already taken off to go home with Theo and Xander. Nancy would soon follow.

"Fern! Fern! Thank God!" Elvis was thrilled to see the girl alive and seemingly well. He emerged from a thicket with Soop, both still holding their long guns. They hustled over to Fern, Diesel leading the way.

Nika could see this from her vantage point. Two men and a dog. Two men with guns, running toward Fern. She let loose a growl and a snarl, fearsome enough to stop a man's heart, and charged from her cover to stop in the clearing. Protective stance.

Soop was the quickest and shouldered his gun to face the big cat.

"DON'T SHOOT!" Fern screamed. Summoning reflexes she hadn't thought possible, she lunged at Carl, grabbed the barrel of his gun, and lifted it up to point to the sky.

Carl looked at Fern and back to the panther. His eyes bugged and his trigger finger twitched.

Elvis was afraid to move. "Fern? What's going on, Fern?"

"Nika, it's okay. It's okay. They are friends," Fern spoke to the panther, ignoring Elvis for the moment.

"Your friend just pointed his gun at me."

"I know, I know. But I stopped him. Trust me please Nika, and I will tell them to trust you."

Elvis and Carl were listening to Fern's end of the conversation with this panther she called Nika. Nothing was normal anymore and they wondered if anything ever would be again.

"Elvis and Carl," Fern began in an instructive and firm voice. "Please very slowly put your guns down on the ground. Please. If you do this she won't attack. If you don't then one of you will die before the other can shoot her. This is one of those times when you absolutely have to make the right decision. Please trust me." Fern glanced over at Nika and knew that she understood what was said to the men. Fern had been talking to the cat as much as she was to Elvis and Carl.

Elvis went first, slowly bending his knees to put his shotgun on the ground. He looked at Fern and then the big cat and then at Carl. "Let's go Soop. We don't have a choice now. That thing is six feet long and about a hundred and fifty pounds of fast."

"I hope you know what you are doing, Fern," Carl said in a low voice. "Something happens to us, and Ma will be super pissed off." He bent low to gently put his rifle down on the grass and then stood back up, hardly believing what he had just done. "Nice pussy cat," he said to Nika without a trace of humor.

"Nika, these are the men from the house where I live with them and their Ma. They are good men. Really good men, but they don't know you and they don't know you were trying to protect me. Ask Pretty about them. We are all friends here."

Diesel didn't want to get involved in a spat between the men and a panther, so he stationed himself next to Pretty. He would jump in to help Elvis and Carl if it came to that, but he desperately hoped it would not.

"Ask Pretty. Ask Delroy. It's all good here. They are nice humans," Fern implored Nika.

Elvis and Carl had just resumed something approaching a regular breathing pattern when Nika began a slow approach to both men. Anxious glances were exchanged between the two men. Nika had her head low, eyes up, and offered a slow growl. "Fern. Tell them this…"

* * *

After a brief confab with the big cat, Fern put an arm around the panther's neck and shoulders and then smiled up at the boys. "Nika says she requires visitation rights. She will be your friend and protect you and fight beside you if she can, just as she did for Copycat. You don't know about that yet, but I'll fill you in later. Anyway, she is a good friend to have as she would be a most fearsome enemy. But you'll need to talk to Ma." Fern paused for a moment to make sure the Pettigrew brothers were listening. "Back me on this. Nika wants visitation rights and I want her to have them too. Nika has to feel safe coming around back at the house without worrying about getting shot."

"Fine with me," Elvis seemed relieved that this was the only condition.

"Fine with me too," Carl agreed. "Super good. I'll talk to Ma, so don't worry about that."

"Diesel, you okay with this?" Elvis wanted to know.

Diesel wagged his tail and went over to Nika. The dog and the cat sniffed at each other and each other's breath, almost touching noses.

"Okay, everybody, let's get out of here. We have to get home before dark and Ma is sick with worry. C'mon Fern, the boat's just over here. Grab your stuff."

Fern was saying a grateful goodbye to Nika and getting whiskers rubbed against her cheek. "I will see you soon," they both said at the same time.

"Pretty, let's go for a ride in the boat," Diesel invited the iguana.

Fern got her backpack, the men got their guns, and just about everybody got into the boat. Nancy flew back to Riverside Estates, Delroy followed the boat from above, and Nika watched the boat ease away from the shoreline.

Fern had Copycat in her arms. "You are such a brave cat, she said.

"Brave cat."

Fern petted Copycat's head. "You must be starving."

"Starving."

"Do you like ice cream? I think Ma has some ice cream."

Copycat's eyes almost bounced out of their sockets like cartoon eyeballs on springs. "Ice cream."

Carl was steering the boat while Elvis called Ma. "I have great news."

Pause

"Fern, yes Fern."

Pause

"She's fine."

Pause

"Ma, she's fine. She's right here. I am looking right at her. We'll be home within the hour."

Pause

"Guess what else, Ma?"

Pause

"We got the cat too!"

Long pause

"Thanks, Ma. So, what's for dinner?"

WE HAD A DEAL

MA WAS HAPPY. The boys had done their job as she'd known they would. She was wrapping up the dishes after serving the wayward bunch a feast of pork chops and mashed potatoes with gravy. Comfort food after a hard couple of days. She peered out the kitchen window and couldn't help but smile. Fern was sitting and chatting with Diesel and Pretty, Copycat licking ice cream from a bowl. The big black vulture was roosted on a low tree, taking it all in. The boys were off to the side, drinking beer and talking business.

"We got your cat." Elvis had Karl on the phone and was smirking at Carl as he spoke. Carl smirked back. "Yeah, I got your cat."

"That's great news, Agnes will be thrilled," Karl said with enough fakery in his voice to win him an Emmy.

"So, I was thinking. This cat cost me a lot of time and money. How much did you say for this cat?" Elvis and Carl were trying not to laugh.

"We agreed on six thousand, Elvis."

"Yeah, but that was before we spent two days and a lot of gas for the boat."

"I don't like this, Elvis. We had a deal," Karl whined.

"Then let's make a new deal. Do you want the cat or not? Think about how happy poor old Agnes will be."

"Sixty-five hundred," tried Karl.

"Seven thousand," Elvis countered. Carl was giggling like a schoolboy.

"Fine. Seven thousand. When do I get the cat?"

"Tomorrow morning."

"Where?"

"We'll meet in the parking lot at Toni's. Eight o'clock. She won't be open yet, so there won't be anyone there. Don't forget the money. Cash. Twenty-dollar bills."

"See you then." Karl wasn't happy about paying more, but he really didn't care all that much. Tomorrow was going to be *big*. Between the cat and the surprise he had planned for his sister, it was going to be a red-letter day.

THE VERY DEFINITION OF VALOR

THEODORE SLOWLY ROLLED into Agnes's driveway and put his SUV in park. He glanced over at Xander and exhaled. "Agnes will be thrilled about Copycat, but the squirrels will have a hard time with the news about Julius. Especially Figaro. They were *very* close."

Xander didn't know what to say.

"Geppetto, stay by Fig and comfort him as well as you can. Tell him how incredibly brave Julius was and how he saved Copycat's life." Theo looked up. "Here they come," he continued as he stepped out onto the driveway.

Agnes took one look at Theo and began to cry. "Oh my God, Theo, are you alright? Look at you! You are a bloody mess. Are you bleeding?" She approached Theo as if to give him a hug and then thought better of it, given his state.

"I'm fine Agnes, really, I'm fine. It's not my blood," Theo said looking down at himself. We found Copycat, Agnes. We found him and he's okay. Unhurt. Fern and the gator-catchers will bring him here first thing tomorrow. He's safe."

"It is quite a story," Xander added.

The squirrels were dancing in circles along with Yogi. Geppetto just watched, waiting for Theo to break the bad news. It hit Figaro first.

"Where's Julius?" Figaro knew something was wrong.

"Come here Fig," Theo said, outstretching his arms.

"No. Tell me where Julius is first." The angst was growing within the red squirrel by the second.

"He is in heaven, Fig. I'm sorry, but Julius isn't with us anymore."

Ripley ran to Figaro, as did Digby. The red was inconsolable.

"He died as he lived, Figaro," Theo said, barely able to get the words out. "With honor and a fierce loyalty to Copycat. He saved Copycat's life from The Big Bad."

Xander looked at Agnes and Agnes looked at Theo. Figaro was not the only one heartbroken. Agnes gave Theo a big warm hug, bloody shirt be damned, and whispered in his ear. "I'm so sorry, Theo. I know you loved that coyote as much as Figaro did."

"Thank you, Agnes. It may take some time to process this, but for now, I need a shower and some clean clothes."

"I agree."

Agnes poured some wine and sat at the patio table with Theo and Xander, listening to their recounting of Julius, Copycat, and The Big Bad; the guns and the panther and the hellish scene that had unfolded. Theo and Xander reassured Agnes that Copycat would be with them soon.

Geppetto and Nancy were telling Figaro about Julius's extraordinary courage in the face of certain death. They had gathered on the back lawn, Geppetto and Nancy and the three squirrels, along with Dante and Elliot. Geppetto had decided that such a tale of bravery would benefit the snake and the frog too, and serve to properly memorialize Julius and establish the legend of the one-eyed coyote who had confronted The Big Bad in his own territory. The very definition of valor.

I SAID TURN AROUND

FERN SAT WITH Pretty and Diesel in front of the Pettigrew house. Copycat in her lap. "You stay here with Ma," she began, addressing the iguana and the dog. "I'm going with the boys to take Copycat back to his home. Behave. I won't be gone long."

The Gators-Be-Gone van was parked in Toni's lot with the flatbed trailer hitched behind it. Elvis and Carl were in front, with Fern holding and petting Copycat in the backseat.

"You'll be home soon."

"Home soon," Copycat purred.

"Here he is," Elvis nodded out the windshield.

"That's him," Carl agreed. "Super nice car he's got."

Karl wheeled his BMW up beside the van and got out.

"Fern, you good?" It was Carl.

"Super good." Fern smiled at her own joke as it sailed right over Carl's head.

"When I open your door, just step out with Copycat. You don't need to say anything. We only want this idiot to see the cat, then you get back inside. Don't let go of the cat for any reason."

"Got it."

"Where's the money?" Elvis said, standing beside the van.

"Where's the cat?"

"We got him. Inside the van. Where's the money? I ain't going to ask you a third time."

Karl appraised the two men. Hard men, but he already knew that. The one called Elvis, the one doing the talking, had his carry weapon holstered in his waistband. The other guy, the *super good* guy, had a savage-looking knife strapped at his side. "It's right here. In my car."

"Let's see it," Carl said.

"Show me the cat first."

Carl had had enough. "You've been watching too much TV mister. This ain't a spy movie. Get the money and I'll get the cat. That's all there is to it."

Karl opened the trunk of his car and produced a duffel bag that looked to be stuffed. "Here," he said, still holding the bag.

"Good." Carl went to the slider door on the van and out came Fern, holding Copycat.

Karl was giddy with excitement. "Great. Here's the money," he said, dropping the bag at Elvis's feet.

Elvis unzipped the bag and grinned like the cat who swallowed the canary. "Looks good. Get back inside, Fern. Thank you."

Fern re-entered the van.

"Hey, wait, give me the cat!" Karl didn't quite understand what was happening.

"Well, we figured since you are doing such a super nice thing for Ms. Agnes - giving her back her cat and all - that we'd like to see the joyous look on her face when she gets her precious pet."

"Yeah," Elvis chimed in. "We want to be there when it happens."

"So," Carl again, "We thought we could give you a lift over there."

Back to Elvis. "No need to thank us, Karl. You paid good money to professionals like me and Soop here to help you find the cat and do this good deed."

"You are one super good guy, Karl. Even if you can't spell your own name," Carl laughed.

Elvis lowered his tone. The fun and games were over. Time for business. "Turn around."

"What?" Karl couldn't believe what was going on.

"I said turn around."

Soop had the zip ties ready.

FIVE MINUTES, TOPS

GERDA AND HER long, lean partner were driving out of
town and heading off to a gas station somewhere,
anywhere but Ashburn. Gerda was wearing her ball cap
and sunglasses to complete what she thought would pass
for a functional disguise.

"You can stay inside the car, Reena. I'll fill up the gas
cans," Gerda said, getting out of her Mercedes after
popping the trunk open.

"Will do." Reena was playing with her phone, checking
Twitter like an obsessive.

Gerda slid her credit card into the gas pump and
started to fill the first of her two cans. She thought that
maybe using her credit card wasn't a good idea, but
probably better than going inside to pay cash. The clerk
would get a good look at her and wonder why she was
paying cash. Nobody does that, do they?

After filling up her gas can with five gallons, Gerda
tried to lift it. Jeez, this is heavy. There is no way I can
carry two. One will have to suffice. I should have thought

about the weight, she chastised herself. No matter. Five gallons will be plenty to get the job done. She put the full can and the empty one back in her trunk and pressed *no receipt* on the pump.

Obeying the speed limit, Gerda and Reena motored along, heading back to Ashburn.

"Nervous?" Gerda glanced over at Reena.

"No. Why would I be?"

"Just checking. We can't have any problems." Another sideways glance. "Let's review."

"We have been over this a dozen times," Reena complained. The conversation was interrupting her phone time. She was doing Wordle and wanted to concentrate.

"One more time." Gerda was getting a little anxious herself. She would be doing the dirty work that night. All Reena had to do was drive.

"Okay, fine." Reena was growing exasperated but put down her phone.

"We go at midnight. You will be dressed as you always are. Just out for a drive in the summer air on a hot night."

"Got it."

"We cruise Sycamore Lane once, just to be sure nobody is out walking their dog."

"At midnight?"

"You never know. Puppies have to pee."

"Okay."

"When the coast is clear, you drop me in the parking lot at the clinic and then take off. Out for a drive. I'll run around the back of the clinic and start dumping gasoline against the side of the building and in the corners. Then I'll run over to Bobnoggin's house and splash the rest of the gas all along the back of his house. I'll light that first and then run back to the clinic to light that up and you will pick me up in the parking lot. Then we hightail it out of there."

"How long do you think this will take you? I can't drive far, Gerda, I'll have to stay close."

"So, stay close. Just don't be parked. I'll be five minutes, tops. As soon as you see flames, come and get me."

"And if something goes wrong? If someone comes along? Should I text you?"

"We won't have our phones with us. We can't have some cell tower ping our phones and place us at the scene. If there is a problem I will run through the backyard and get to the golf course. Meet me in the maintenance shed parking area. I can wait for you there. Got it? If I don't see you at the clinic lot then I will bolt across the creek to the golf course. If you don't see me, same thing. Go to the golf course. That's our back-up rendezvous."

"Okay. This seems simple enough." Reena was nodding her head.

"All you have to do is drive and be there when I need you. We can swing by the crappy diner on Washington Street and dump the gas cans and the rest of the stuff in the dumpster behind it."

Reena smiled. "This might even be fun. Just like on TV!"

A COUPLE OF GOOD MEN

"ASHBURN POLICE, HOW may I direct your call?"

"Detective Donovan, please."

"May I tell him who's calling?

"Bruno Fischer. He knows me."

"One moment."

"Bruno. Hi, how are you?"

"I'm fine, Jay. How about you?

"Good. All good."

"That's good to hear. How about Anne, she good?"

"Yeah. She's fine. The kids are running her ragged, but you know how it is. So, what's up?"

"Jay, I have certain knowledge from an anonymous source. There will be an attempted arson tonight."

"Arson?"

"Yeah, arson," Bruno confirmed.

Detective Jay Donovan sipped his coffee. "Bruno, you are contracts and civil litigation. Maybe real estate, but not criminal. Why is a business lawyer calling me about an arson? And how the hell do you know about this?"

"I told you," Bruno sipped his own coffee. "An anonymous source." He smiled to himself. Jay would figure it out soon enough.

Donovan fumbled around for a pen. "Okay. Give me the details. This better be good, Bruno. I can't have my guys running around on a wild goose chase. We are short on resources as it is."

Bruno leaned back in his office chair. "You ready?"

"Ready."

"The target site is the Doctor Nichole Florentine Animal Clinic on Sycamore Lane."

"What? Why would anyone want to burn that place down?"

"The other target site is Theodore Bobnoggin's house next door to the clinic."

"Are you kidding me?" The detective was in a state of disbelief. "What kind of idiot would want to do that?"

"Gerda Snell."

"Snell?"

"Yup. Snell. Karl Snell's sister. You remember him, don't you?"

"Of course I do. I thought he left town?"

"He did. He's in Florida."

Jay thought about this, rubbing his forehead. Karl Snell is a snake and, apparently so is his sister. What are the Snells up to? There might be more to this than meets the eye. "Bruno, I'm going to call you back. Let me see who is on tonight and who I might need to call in. Just give me five minutes. I'll call you right back."

Jay Donovan leaned in his chair and put his feet on his desk. Gerda Snell. Karl Snell's sister. Unreal. Herman must be behind this. He left his office to check the duty roster for the night shift. Vic Benton. Good. He's reliable. I'll send Mike Rossi as backup. Rossi can drop Vic off at the site and then park the cruiser somewhere and come back. They will have to hide out behind some trees or something. Can't have police cars out front or nothing will happen and they will come up empty. They will have to catch her in the act and *before* she lights the match.

Jay called Bruno, as promised. "Okay. I have a couple of good men I can send over to stake it out. No cars, no lights. I'll put them in night gear and hide them in the back of the house and the clinic. You had better be right about this, Bruno. Don't make a fool of me in front of my men. This has to be real."

"It's real."

NO FIRE, ONLY ICE

THE GATORS-BE-GONE VAN was halfway to Agnes's house when Fern called the number on the poster. "Hello, Agnes?"

"Yes?"

"It's Fern. We have Copycat, he is safe and unharmed. We'll be there in ten minutes."

"Oh, Fred. My precious Fred."

Fern put her phone on speaker. "Say hello, Copycat. Say hello."

"Hello."

"Did you hear that, Agnes?"

"No."

"That's okay. We'll be there soon."

The welcoming party included everyone. Theo and the squirrels, Geppetto and Nancy on a low branch of the live oak. Xander and Yogi. Even Dante had slithered up to watch. Agnes was front and center on the driveway.

The van with its trailer eased up in front of the house.

Fern was the first one out, Copycat in her arms. "Go,

Copycat, go."

Copycat missile-launched out of Fern's arms and into Agnes's awaiting embrace.

"Oh, my Fred, my special Fred." Agnes was sobbing. "My Fred."

The squirrels cried, their heads bobbing up and down. Rip, Fig, and Dig. Geppetto bird-hopped along the tree branch, a few inches closer to Nancy. Xander looked down at Yogi, who looked up at Xander. Love. Dante did nothing because snakes do not emote unless threatened or angry. (At least not that anybody could tell.) Theo gave Agnes an appropriate moment and then opened his arms in a wide embrace of his friend and her beloved cat. His beloved cat. *Their* heroic cat.

"Gentlemen, I can't thank you enough. And you, Fern. We will be forever grateful. We owe you." Theo glanced around and everyone nodded in agreement.

Agnes moved toward the two gator wranglers and hugged them both. Holding for a moment because it was real. Then Fern. A long, heartfelt hug of the utmost sincerity. "I will not ever forget what you have done for me."

"Well, this party ain't over yet," Carl said with much glee. "We got another surprise for you."

"Yup," Elvis agreed and went over to the trailer hitched to the back of the van. "Ladies and gentlemen," he looked around, "and animals. I would like to present to you, Mr. Karl Snell."

Carl went to the trailer and tore off the tarp on the trailer. "Here he is, my super good friend, Karl with a K. Except he's so stupid he can't spell his own name."

Karl was splayed across the flatbed trailer, hands and

feet zip-tied, and a filthy rag stuffed in his mouth.

"Unnnhh. Arrgh. Umnnuth."

Carl was having too much fun. "Here, let me help you with that, my friend." He took the rag from Karl's mouth.

Karl spat, and spat some more, before looking at the assemblage before him.

Theo and Xander and Agnes were agape. As were the animals.

"Snell? *Snell*? What are you doing here?" Theo was astonished.

"Allow me to explain," started Elvis. "This here moron offered us seven thousand dollars for your cat."

The entire gathering was stunned.

"He said he wanted to bring the cat back to Agnes. But me and Soop didn't believe him. So, we took his money and brought him along for the ride. Bringing the cat back to Agnes."

"Wait a second." It was Theo. "He offered you seven thousand dollars for Copycat?"

"Yup."

"Why?"

"Well, we figured he was going to kill it and send it to you in a box."

If a collective malfunction of thought could occur, this was it. All were speechless. At least for a moment.

Figaro jumped on the trailer and started screeching the way only an enraged squirrel could.

Fern ran over to be with Fig. To face Snell.

Karl was beside himself. He knew he was in trouble deep. He scooched back in the trailer as far as he could, staring wide-eyed at the red squirrel. "What is he doing? What is he saying?"

"He says he wants to eat your eyeballs. Well, sort of. He

was a lot more graphic than that." Fern smiled.

"My eyeballs? My eyeballs?"

"Well, yes."

Karl started whining and mewling. "Let me go. I'm going to call the cops!"

Dante had managed to slither up onto the back of the trailer. He wasn't quite sure what was going on, but Figaro had a clear distaste for the shouty human. That was all the snake needed to know. He flickered his tongue in the most menacing way he could conjure. "I am a Florida cottonmouth, and I am lethal. My venom would paralyze and consume you with pain. I am the most skilled assassin in the land."

Theo stepped up. "Enough, Dante. Thanks, but he doesn't understand you. I think he still gets the point."

Elvis had had his fill of Karl with a K. "You ain't calling nobody."

Theo had also had enough. He approached Karl with fire in his eyes and said, "Karl, you are done here."

Karl, oblivious to his circumstances, continued, "I'm calling the cops."

Carl sauntered over to Karl and, faster than fast, whipped out his knife and said, "Don't move."

Carl snipped the zip tie around Karl's feet with not much more than a twitch with his blade. "Now, don't you move, mister." He then flicked his knife to sever the zip tie around Karl's wrists. Carl stood back. "You are free to go, asshole."

"I'm still going to call the cops."

Xander had seen false bravado before. He also knew enough to know, that you never *really* know. Maybe he *will* call the cops? "Excuse me," he said edging his way around Theo and Carl. He leaned in toward Karl. His face, passive and flat, no emotion, just *truth*, inches from Karl's nose.

Karl looked into Xander's eyes and saw no fire, only ice.

Xander spoke in a low voice, through his teeth. "I have spent decades in darkness. I have done the darkest of things. I am a ghost. And I will slit your throat while you sleep."

Karl came very close to losing his bladder.

Xander stood erect and launched a broad smile at all those gathered. "Don't worry. He's not going to call the cops."

Karl scrambled to the edge of the trailer and stopped. "What about my money?"

Elvis and Carl shook their heads. This guy really is stupid.

"You know what?" Carl began. "You are not a Karl. You don't deserve to be a Karl. Even if you could spell it right." He doubled over in laughter at his own joke.

Elvis said, "You know what, Carl? You're right." Elvis was beaming. "Hey Karl, we did our job. You hired us to catch that cat, and we did. You said you wanted Agnes to have the cat back, and she does. You said you wanted to bring it to her, and you did. We just gave you a ride, that's all."

Carl wanted to pile on. "Yeah. Mission accomplished. That money's ours. We earned it. Now go, start running. Run Karl, run!"

That is exactly what Karl did. He ran to the end of the street in his rumpled and dirty suit, looked left and then right, and took off as fast as his legs would carry him.

Everybody watched, and everybody laughed. The gang was back together, safe and happy. If only Julius could have enjoyed the moment with them.

The back patio was waiting. Coffee and croissants. Ice

cream for Copycat. Grapes for Geppetto. Nancy declined the offer. Grapes?

HIS MONEY WAS GONE

KARL MADE IT back to Toni's parking lot in a taxi and stood looking at his lonely BMW. The sun was baking the exterior and the interior was hotter than a Sicilian pizza oven. He turned the ignition on and put the air conditioning on max. Too hot to sit inside, he paced back and forth beside his car, waiting for the climate control settings to do their job. He was furious. Those guys stole my money! Calling the cops wasn't going to get him anywhere - how could he explain the whole escapade without implicating himself? It would be like complaining to the police about a drug deal gone bad. Besides, there was that tall, *slit-your-throat* guy to worry about. Don't want to go there. That guy was a little too real.

No matter. His seven thousand dollars were gone, but there was plenty more where that came from. Besides, he still had a nice steak dinner and lots of excitement to look forward to tonight. Big sister was going down. The car had finally cooled somewhat, so he got in and took off back to his condo in Orlando.

* * *

Karl grabbed a cut crystal, double old-fashioned from his cabinet and scanned his bar cart. Maybe bourbon this time. The good stuff. He opened a bottle of twenty-year-old Pappy Van Winkle. It was about a hundred dollars a sip, but he figured he had earned it after what he'd just been through. One gulp. Another. He made his way into his bedroom where he disrobed before going into the shower. His suit was ruined, so he threw it in a heap in the corner. All he could think of for the time being was to wash off the dead animal stink from that red-neck, huckleberry trailer.

Sipping on another bourbon, slowly this time, Karl, out of the shower and still naked, surveyed the suits in his closet. What shall I wear tonight? Armani? Brioni? No, let's go with American. Ralph Lauren, Purple Label. This night was going to be the most fun he had had in a long time.

COP STUFF

DETECTIVE JAY DONOVAN pressed the button on his rearview mirror to open the garage door and then parked inside. He paused for a minute, thinking. Gerda Snell was supposedly going to burn down the animal clinic on Sycamore Lane and Bobnoggin's house along with it. He was conflicted in the extreme. He considered his options, failed to come to a satisfactory conclusion, and went inside.

"Hey sweetheart," Jay greeted his wife in the kitchen.

"Hey, Jay," she responded as she always did. She liked the rhyme. "What's going on?"

"Cop stuff. Same old." Jay spied his two kids at the kitchen table. Both seemingly doing homework. "Hi, guys. What are you doing? What's going on?"

Jack, twelve years old, replied, "Homework, what else?"

"Hi, Daddy!" Cara, nine, said. "Homework for me too."

"Well okay, then." Jay gave his wife a married-for-years hug and a kiss on the cheek. "What's for dinner?"

"Pizza puffs and mac & cheese."

"Why am I not surprised?" Jay looked over at his son. "Jack, you can't have pizza puffs all the time. You need some variety in your diet."

"Why?"

"Cara. You too. You can't have mac and cheese every night."

"Why not?"

"Because it's not healthy, that's why."

"Mac and cheese has protein and carbs. It's healthy." Cara was sure of herself.

"Well, maybe a vegetable once in a while might be good."

"Vegetables are for grown-ups."

With the kids fully involved in their meal, Jay wondered what might be in the offing for him. "So, what's for us?" He looked at his wife. The wife he was way too lucky to have.

Anne put on her oven mitts and pulled out a casserole dish from the oven. "Leftover lasagna."

Jay was thrilled. His wife's leftover lasagna would be, hard to believe, even better than the original.

"Listen, Jay," Anne ventured, "There was another round of layoffs at work today. Not really a surprise. You know how it is. Downsizing, re-purposing, and all that crap."

Jay stiffened. "How does this affect you?"

"Well, other than some good friends getting screwed, it doesn't. But I am on the block, I can see it coming."

Jay thought about this and then thought some more.

"Don't worry, Anne. We'll be fine." Jay hugged his wife in a very real and warm way. "I've got us covered. Always have, always will."

* * *

After the dinner dishes were cleared, rinsed, and in the dishwasher, Jay said to his wife, "I have to go out."

"What for?"

"Cop stuff. I'll be back in an hour."

It took two.

Sitting in his car, after an excruciating wait in the Starbucks drive-through, Jay thumbed his phone. Then stopped himself. Am I really going to do this?

LET ME ENJOY MY DRINK FIRST

LONNY'S WAS PACKED. Mostly with a lot of tourists from *up north*, but some who have settled.

Karl valet parked his car and, standing for a minute or two at the entrance to the best steakhouse for miles, he gazed in wonderment at the license plates in the train of cars easing into the valet line. New York, New Jersey, Pennsylvania. One or two from Ontario, Canada. The great migration, he thought. Money from *up north*, coming south to escape the cold. Coming to Florida where there is no state income tax. He couldn't blame them.

Inside he told the hostess he would be eating at the bar and proceeded to find a good seat. He had a view of the windows, a partial view of the main dining room, and a view of the front entrance so he could people-watch and judge them all. Assessing their comportment and their sartorial failings. Look at that guy's cheap shoes. His off-the-rack suit doesn't fit. Her hair is offensive. Karl was having fun. He felt superior when he criticized others. Which was all the time.

"What can I get you?" the bartender asked as he put

down a cocktail napkin in front of Karl.

"You *may* get me a vodka martini, thanks. Grey Goose, two olives, slightly dirty."

The bartender turned to shake up a martini for the snotty guy at the bar. "Here you go. Would you like a menu?"

"I would, but not yet. Let me enjoy my drink first."

Karl did just that. He enjoyed his martini immensely while one half of his brain was watching the unwashed come and go and the other half was making a movie in his head. He was picturing the look on Gerda's face when she got busted by the cops in Ashburn. He was also picturing the look on his father's face when he found out that his plan had failed. Karl smirked to himself while he played and replayed the video in his mind. I am doing the right thing, he told himself. I am preventing a major crime. Maybe I'm not so bad after all. Who would want to see an animal clinic go up in flames?

He had his phone on the polished hardwood bar and saw it light up. It was his father. I'll let that go to voice mail. A minute later he got a text. *I hope you are at Lonny's like I told you.* Yup, I sure am. And I won't forget to expense what will surely be a delicious meal.

Karl asked for the menu and a wine list. It didn't take long. "I'll have the bone-in ribeye, with bordelaise, and a baked potato."

"How would you like your steak prepared, sir."

"Rare."

"Very good, sir."

"Oh, and I will have a glass of your Opus One cabernet."

"I'm very sorry, but that is only available by the

bottle."

"So, bring me the whole damn bottle."

The steak was good. Better than good, and so was the wine. Karl looked at his phone and decided to just turn it off. He didn't want to hear anything or know anything until tomorrow.

LET'S GO

GERDA AND REENA were relaxing at home in Gerda's condo. Or, at least they were trying to. Both were nervous, but that's what makes it fun, no?

Finally, Gerda stood. "Let's go."

"Why? It's only eleven o'clock."

"C'mon, let's go. We can drive around for a bit. I'm getting way too antsy just sitting here."

Reena unwound herself from the sofa. "Okay. Let's get your backpack ready."

"It's ready now." Gerda went into the bedroom and returned with a black Patagonia pack, stuffed with everything she would need other than the gas can, which was waiting in the trunk of her car.

"Cell phone, please," Gerda addressed Reena, holding out her hand.

"Seriously?"

"We have been through this. No phones." Gerda allowed some measure of impatience in her voice. She put her own phone on the kitchen counter. "We can't be placed at the scene. We need to be established as being at home."

Reena put her phone on the counter, not at all convinced about the "no phones" part of the plan. "What happens if something goes wrong? What if I need to call you?"

"Nothing is going to go wrong. And if something does, I sure as hell don't want you calling me." Gerda caught Reena's eyes and didn't let go. "We have gone through this a thousand times. When you see fire or smoke, you come and get me in the parking lot at the animal clinic. Our backup is the golf course. Please tell me you've got this."

Reena nodded, thinking that maybe Gerda shouldn't be using that tone of voice with her.

Together they went down in the elevator, into the parking garage, and got in the car.

Reena's phone never did get pinged. Gerda's phone was pinged. More than once.

CALL IT OFF

JAY FINALLY MADE a decision. In the Starbucks parking lot, heart racing, he made the call. One way or another, nobody was setting fire to anything.

From his contact list, Jay checked a number he hadn't thought he would need again.

Herman Snell was lounging in his Natuzzi recliner and was playing the game in his head. Play the game or the game plays you. He was always a step ahead. His mind was bifurcated or trifurcated, at all times. Calculating if-then scenarios. Checking his phone like an obsessive. Overseas markets and NYSE stock market futures. What would the financial markets do tomorrow? His thoughts were disturbed by his phone lighting up. What?

"Hello?"

"Herman. It's Jay Donovan. Detective Donovan."

Herman's heart skipped a beat. "I know who you are. Why are you calling me?"

"I'm calling to do you a favor, Herman. And I'm sort of

thinking you might want to compensate me for that favor."

Oh no. Oh shit. Herman could think of nothing other than the possibility of his plan gone awry. A cop calling me from Ashburn? He glanced at his Rolex. Too early. Nothing has happened yet.

"What is it, Donovan?" Herman was leaning forward in his chair now, his full attention on the detective's voice.

"I don't know what you're thinking Herman, and don't tell me, I don't want to know. Trust me. Just listen." Jay was nervous about asking for money, but this was his chance. "You and I have done a few small favors for each other in the past, but this is a big one. I hope you see it that way." Jay felt as if he were juggling chainsaws.

"I'm listening."

"Call it off, Herman. This thing tonight."

"How do you know about this *thing* tonight?"

"I just do. I'm a detective, Herman. I know things. I have informants."

Herman's mind was racing. How does he know this? Did Gerda talk? Has she opened her stupid mouth?

"Look," Jay continued, "I have certain knowledge of a major crime that is being planned for tonight. I have men at the site. I have to act. If I don't act and this thing goes down, my informant will wonder why I did nothing to stop it. I can't have that. This is my job. I don't want to see anything go up in flames, Herman. I can't just let that happen. So, I'm trying to save your ass and your daughter's ass. Call it off. No harm, no foul."

Herman glanced at his watch again. He was starting to sweat. There's still time. "Alright, Jay. I appreciate the call. I don't know how to thank you."

"Yes, you do. You know damn well how to thank me."

Juggling chainsaws.

Herman stood and paced in tight circles before snatching up his phone and stabbing furiously at it.

RADIO SILENCE

OFFICER MIKE ROSSI was driving an unmarked car from the station pool. Officer Vic Benton was riding shotgun as they approached Sycamore Lane.

"We're kind of early, don't you think?" Benton looked at Rossi.

"It's not the sort of thing we want to be late for, Vic. Seriously, we don't want to screw this up."

"I guess you're right." Vic Benton checked his pockets and poked inside his backpack, making sure he hadn't forgotten anything. Water, a protein bar, a black balaclava and night vision goggles. "You got your night eyes, Mike?"

"Yeah. In the back." Rossi turned the corner onto Sycamore Lane and did a slow pass in front of the animal clinic and then the Bobnoggin residence. Nothing. "It looks pretty quiet, Vic. You jump here and station in some tree cover behind the house. I will park back around the corner and run back to set up behind the clinic. This might be a long wait, so get comfortable."

"Got it," Vic said. "Radio silence, right?"

"Yup. If you need to tell me anything, shade your phone

and text me."

With night vision better than anything the cops might have, Hendrix wondered at the goings on at Doc Nicky's clinic and behind Theo's house. Two humans. Both with strange equipment, dark clothes, and funny-looking goggles on their heads. Something's not right. Something's happening. He floated down, in absolute silence, to a perch on the giant white oak in Theo's backyard. Central to the sanctuary grounds he was sworn to protect. His owl senses told him that these two humans were not a threat. There was another threat, not yet seen. What are they hiding from? Hendrix decided to wait and see what might develop.

NO DOG WALKERS

REENA WAS BEHIND the wheel, as planned. She and Gerda did a slow roll down Sycamore Lane. All quiet. No dog walkers.

Gerda glanced at the dashboard clock. Just a little after midnight - time to go. "All right, Reena. We'll be drinking wine at home soon. Let's do this."

Reena looped around the far end of Sycamore Lane and drove slowly back to the clinic, headlights off. In the lot, the two co-conspirators exchanged a *good luck* look and Gerda opened her door. "Five minutes max. Probably three." Gerda took a deep breath and exhaled. She didn't bother to close her door quietly, nor did she make an effort to close the trunk lid quietly. If anybody was around, they'd already been spotted.

Reena winced at the racket Gerda was making and watched her lumber through the lot, weighed down by her backpack and the heavy gas can. Time to leave. Reena exited the parking lot and, once again, did a slow roll down the lane.

* * *

Vic texted Mike: "Car."
Mike texted back: "Heard."

ABORT!

HERMAN HELD HIS phone in a white-knuckled grip, listening to the rings on the other end. Counting them. Voice mail. "Answer the phone, Gerda. Answer the phone!" He clicked off and waited for the callback. No callback.

He called again, voice mail again. A different approach. "Gerda, sweetie, call me back right away. I know you're *busy*, but this is important. Please call me back as soon as you get this. Thanks."

Herman stomped around his living room, staring at his phone as if *willing* it to ring. C'mon, c'mon, call me.

No call. Herman had trouble processing the lack of response. He called again, voice mail again. He screamed into the microphone. "Stand down! Do you hear me? Stand down! ABORT! ABORT!"

He waited fifteen excruciating minutes before calling again. "Listen to me you little bitch, when I call you, you answer the phone. This is not optional, so wrap your pea brain around that. Abort your mission and call me to confirm."

* * *

Herman popped a Xanax and spent the rest of his evening gazing at his phone until he passed out. Alcohol and drug-induced oblivion. His phone stayed silent.

SHOT FIRED

VIC AND MIKE were each looking at a green world through their night vision goggles. They readied their service weapons as they watched a clumsy woman drag a gas can to the rear of the clinic. They had both thought this stakeout would be a waste of time - bad info from an anonymous source - but here she was. Unbelievable. Somebody was actually going to try to burn down the animal clinic.

Mike tossed his goggles to the side and bolted from his hiding spot as the woman started to splash gasoline against the side of the building. The air was pungent with the incendiary.

Vic also dumped his goggles and raced out from behind a tree.

Both men were fast but not faster than Hendrix. The great horned owl streaked in from the night sky and, with his three-inch talons, tore the White Sox baseball cap from Gerda's head, leaving a bloody gash on her scalp.

Gerda screamed and dropped the gas can. She clutched at her wounded head and withdrew her hands to see them covered in blood. She didn't quite understand what had happened. A bird? A bird would ruin her plans? It's okay. Okay. Okay, she told herself. Breathing hard. I can still do this. Reena can play nurse back at home.

"Freeze!" It was Mike, gun drawn. "Don't move. Slow, really slow, show me your hands and get on your knees."

Gerda simply couldn't think fast enough to make a good decision. So, she made a bad one. She reached into her backpack and pulled out the butane lighter wand.

"Freeze!" It was Vic this time. "Drop the lighter."

Mike Rossi was never, ever, going to shoot an unarmed woman. But he thought about it. Vic Benton was a certified firearms instructor and an expert marksman. He thought about it too.

Gerda was panicked. "Drop your guns, or I will light this place up!" She was waving around the lighter.

That's all Vic needed to hear. He fired a 9mm round straight through the lighter in Gerda's hand. The lighter went flying. So did Gerda's thumb. Gerda screamed. Mike tackled her, cuffed her, and asked her what she was thinking.

Vic was on his radio. "Shot fired. We need an ambulance and a duty supervisor. Behind the animal clinic on Sycamore Lane."

THE EASY DECISION

REENA HAD NOT been far away. She had the windows of the Mercedes Benz rolled down so she might hear if anything was happening. There was a lot happening. She heard Gerda scream. Loud voices. A gunshot. More screaming. That was all she needed to hear. There would be no pick-up at the clinic and there would be no emergency extraction at the golf course. Nope. None of that.

She made the easy decision to drive. Just drive. She would leave her cell phone behind at the condo, and she would leave Gerda behind at the scene of her crime. This was a whole lot more than she had bargained for.

She tapped at the NAV map function on the car's touch screen and made her way to the highway. Screw this. She was headed back to Boston.

SHE'S TALKING

HERMAN WOKE UP in his reclining chair, still dressed in his suit from the night before - his head a foggy mess. He scanned his living room, just to be sure where he was. Reality landed on him with a sickening thud. He picked up his phone and stared at it. No calls.

He stood and tried to piece things together when his phone buzzed. It wasn't Gerda.

"Herman, you are a complete asshole. I tried to warn you."

"What? Jay?"

"Yes, it's Jay. Who else would call you from this number? Listen to me, Herman. Gerda is in the hospital. She has a gash on her head, but that's not the worst of it. She was shot in the hand by one of my men. She'll live, but she's under arrest for attempted arson, threatening a police officer and a whole lot more stuff it would take too long to tell you. She's in deep trouble. And she's talking. That means you, sir, are also in deep trouble. Do you understand what I'm telling you?"

Herman did. Sort of. "Gerda's talking?"

"She is implicating you as the mastermind of this folly. She wants a plea deal and she's going to get one. You, Herman, have a serious problem. You need to do something, go somewhere, I don't know where, but you need to do it fast."

Herman was frozen, not moving. "Umm, okay."

Jay lowered his phone, away from his face, raised it back up again, and sighed. "This is the second favor I'm doing for you in two days. I hope you will remember that when it comes time to pay your debts." He was juggling chainsaws yet again.

"I'll take care of you."

Herman raced into the shower to clean up, then dress. He grabbed a carry-on roller bag, stuffed it with a few essentials, and then picked up an empty workout bag. I need to stop at the office, he thought. Risky, but I have to. I need to get all that cash that's in my office safe.

A WOMAN IN CUSTODY

KARL SLEPT PAST his alarm. He slept the sleep of the damned when the damned just don't care. The only reason he got up, was to pee. Getting older, he thought. He skipped his morning workout, brewed a pot of coffee, and settled in at his kitchen counter to nurse his hangover and consider his next steps. He didn't know what had happened the night before, but he was dying to find out. He checked his phone. Nothing. Good. He flipped open his laptop and fired up the internet.

The local news in Ashburn was pretty quick. The good journalists that they are, they followed police scanner activity and were sure to disseminate anything gossip-worthy to the good citizens of their fair town.

Attempted arson at the Dr. Nichole Florentine Animal Clinic and Bobnoggin Wildlife Sanctuary on Sycamore Lane. Shots fired. Fire trucks and ambulances were called to the scene. A woman was in custody under suicide watch at the hospital. Gerda Snell, the daughter of prominent businessman, Herman Snell, is the person of interest. Residents are shocked. The officers on the scene are on mandatory desk duty pending a full investigation. This is still a developing story. More details to follow as they become available.

Karl stood and backed away from the counter. He was on the verge of dancing a jig, but managed to control himself. Just barely. He was smiling so broadly that he had to smack himself on the cheeks. His plan was working. Now, what about his father? What was he going to do?

As if on cue, his phone buzzed. It was his father leaving a text message. *You are in charge until I get back.*

Get back? Where was he going? Things could not have been better for Karl. He couldn't believe his luck.

I'M CALLING MY LAWYER

TWO UNIFORMED ORLANDO police officers sat in their unmarked car in the parking lot, in front of the Precept Realty building. Waiting for Herman Snell to arrive at his office. In the back seat was a third, a sour-faced man in a suit. Special Agent Somebody from the Orlando field office of the FBI. He didn't talk much, but the two cops did.

"So, do we nab him outside? In the parking lot?" Officer Lou Rodriguez asked his partner.

"Why? We got a search warrant for his office. Might as well take a look." Officer James Harkness replied. "I'd rather get him inside. See what's up. Safer anyway. He'll be contained in case he gets stupid."

"Yeah, I guess you're right." Rodriguez looked in his rearview mirror. "What do you think, Mr. FBI man?"

No response.

"Outside, or inside?

"Inside." The FBI man caught the officer's eyes in the mirror.

Rodriguez and Harkness agreed. Nodding. It would be more fun to nab him inside. Make him do a perp walk in

244

cuffs and in front of his staff. Cool.

The three men fell into playing with their phones and sipping barely warm coffee. "Here he is," Rodriguez said.

All three watched Herman Snell walk into the building with a small gym bag. A gym bag? I wonder where he thinks he's going? The collective thought.

Herman got off the elevator and barked at Marcy. "Panama. This morning. As soon as possible. See what you can get me." He strode into his office and slammed his door shut.

"Sure thing," Marcy said to empty space, wondering what this was all about. She bent over her keyboard and began clacking at a hundred miles per hour.

Herman plopped into his chair behind his desk, wondering how much time he had. He logged in to his computer and began deleting his emails as fast as he could. There were a lot of them. Before he was finished, he realized that Marcy probably had them all stored in the cloud anyway, so he was wasting his time.

Get the cash. His wall safe hidden behind a still-life painting of some flowers in a vase. A copy of something. The painting was mounted on hinges to swing open to reveal the safe door behind it. Just like in the movies.

Marcy entered without knocking. "Orlando to Panama City at 11:15, but you have to fly coach on United. I can get you in first class on COPA Airlines, but that flight doesn't leave until late this afternoon."

"Get me on the United flight, I don't care about coach. Just book me on that flight and send the info and boarding pass to my phone." Herman started working the dial on his safe. He messed up the combination and had to start again. Jittery. Going too fast. Slow down and everything will be fine.

Marcy closed the door behind her, went to her desk, and looked up to see three men approach. Two cops and some other guy in a brown suit. "May I help you?" Herman was going down and there was no way out of it now.

"I'm Officer Rodriguez and this is," motioning to one side, "Officer Harkness." He put on a friendly face and continued, "This is…"

The man in the brown suit and military haircut, high and tight, pulled an identification wallet from an inside breast pocket and flashed his badge. Marcy caught a glimpse of his gun in a shoulder harness. "FBI." That was it. No name was offered. Just "FBI."

"We have a warrant for the arrest of Herman Snell. Is he in?" Don't lie to me sweetie, thought Rodriguez, but didn't say.

"We also have a search warrant." Harkness waved around an envelope and smiled.

"Follow me," Marcy said, cheerily. She walked the men to Herman's office where she opened the door. "Herman, these men are here to see you." She almost snickered as she spoke the words.

Herman fixed still, one hand reaching into his safe for a stack of bills, the other hand holding his gym bag. He recovered from his frozen posture and stood erect. "Who are you? What do you want?" As if he didn't know.

Rodriguez took the lead. "Herman Snell, we have a warrant for your arrest."

"A warrant?"

"Actually, two of them. We have a search warrant also," Harkness amended.

The FBI guy stood back and stayed close to the door. Just in case Herman tried to bolt.

"Do you know who I am?" Herman protested.

Rodriguez and Harkness looked at each other. "Yeah. Herman Snell."

"I'm calling my lawyer."

"Not yet," said Rodriguez. "First, you're going to turn around so I can cuff you. And you are *not* going to resist, correct?"

Harkness jumped in. He liked this part. "You have the right to remain silent. Anything you say can and will be used against you in a court of law. You with me so far, Herman? You have the right to an attorney. Got that, Herman? If you cannot afford an attorney, one will be provided for you. Do you understand these rights I have just read to you?"

"Yes," Herman whimpered.

"With these rights in mind, do you wish to speak to me?"

"No."

On the way out, Herman turned to Marcy, and in a remarkable display of cognitive failure, barked, "Karl is in charge until I get back. Got it?"

"Got it," Marcy agreed, thinking that Herman might not be back for a long time.

DID YOU CRY?

THEO WAS BREAKFASTING with Agnes and the crew, enjoying a second cup of coffee and a second stack of pancakes with maple syrup. "These are delicious, Agnes. Your hospitality has been overwhelming."

"I'm just so happy you could visit, Nogs. It has been too long."

Theo swallowed a mouthful. "It has been quite a trip. And not uneventful to say the least."

"You are a hero, Nogs. Don't forget that because nobody else will." Agnes knew Theo was stinging from the loss of Julius, but there was little she could do. She knew also that time heals all wounds.

Xander wandered over with Yogi in tow. "Good morning!"

"Good morning, Xander," Theo and Agnes said in unison.

"Any more pancakes?"

"No," Agnes smiled. "Theo ate them all."

"Ha! Figures." Xander sat with them for a coffee while Yogi padded over to check in with the squirrels and

Copycat. "So, you are leaving tomorrow Theo?"

Theo sat back in his chair. "Yeah, tomorrow morning." He knew it would be emotional. "But first we have a party at Ma Pettigrew's tonight. Soop and Elvis say she will be prepping and cooking all day, so we had better show up hungry."

Xander rubbed his chin. "That sounds pretty good." He paused for a second. "Everybody is invited?"

"That's what they said. The three of us, plus Yogi, Copycat, the squirrels, and the birds. Everybody. Fern has guaranteed their safety."

Xander and Agnes nodded, thinking about this. From what?

"I think we can leave Dante behind," Theo added.

Xander and Agnes nodded again. Good idea.

Theo's phone vibrated in his pocket. He looked. "Excuse me," he said, getting up. "I'm going to take this call. It's Nicky."

"Hi, Nicky. How are you?"

"I'm fine, Theo. Thankfully."

"Thankfully? What does that mean? What's going on up there? Are you okay?" Concern crept into Theo's voice.

"I'm good. All good. How are things down there? I haven't heard from you in a couple of days."

"Well, there has been a lot going on." Theo was dreading telling Nicky about Julius. "So, tell me. What is happening up there?"

"A lot is happening, Theo. A lot."

"You go first." Theo was still concerned. A lot?

"Theo, there was an attempted arson last night at the clinic."

Theo's face dropped. "Arson? What?"

"Don't worry, there was no fire, nothing happened. Well, other than Gerda Snell getting shot by the police."

Theo dropped his phone, coughed, and picked it back up. "Sorry. What? Gerda Snell? Karl's sister?"

"Yes. That Gerda Snell. The cops apparently had an anonymous tip and waited behind the clinic. She was going to burn down your house as well. That's what the cops said. She's in the hospital now. They shot her in the hand."

"You've got to be kidding me." Theo was flabbergasted.

"No. Not kidding. They also said a large bird flew down and ripped open a gash in her scalp. I'm guessing that was Hendrix."

Hendrix. Doing his job. "But you're okay. Right?"

"Yeah, I'm fine. A little shaken and stirred, but fine. I didn't know anything about it until this morning when some detective rang my doorbell. He says I'll need a remediation crew to go to the clinic to clean up all the spilled gasoline. I think I can get that done today."

"All right, well, this is a lot to process, but you are okay and that's all that counts."

"Theo?"

"Yes?"

"Don't tell the others until you get home. Copycat and the squirrels will just be unnecessarily upset. So don't say anything for now. Especially to Julius. You know how he gets.

Theo had known this moment would come and he hated it. "Nicky?"

"Yes?"

"About Julius."

Theodore told Doc Nicky about the heroism of her

beloved coyote. The one-eyed coyote she had ministered to on several occasions at her clinic. Her special Julius. The coyote she had scolded to stop fighting and getting into scrapes. The coyote who wouldn't listen because there always seemed to be a friend in need. The coyote Theo had once pretended was his dog. Julius.

"I'm sorry to tell you this on the phone, Nicky. I didn't want to arrive home and surprise you without Julius."

"I understand, Theo."

A moment of silence.

"I'm leaving tomorrow morning and will probably drive straight through. So, I'll see you in a couple of days."

"I can't wait. You drive carefully, please."

Another moment of silence.

"I love you."

"I love you too, Theo."

Silence.

"Theo?"

"Yes?"

"Did you cry?"

"Yes."

Nicky felt her throat tighten. "I believe I will too."

SILENT GOODBYES

THEO AND XANDER had been riding around in Xander's golf cart and drinking beer for a chunk of the afternoon. It was decided that it would be a good idea for Agnes to drive to the party at Ma's. In Theo's brand-new Audi, no less. It was a white-knuckle drive, but they made it.

It was like a carnival jalopy, with innumerable pranksters piling out of the car. Three humans, three squirrels, a cat, and a dog. Geppetto and Nancy had decided to fly on their own after learning that Agnes would be driving.

Diesel and Pretty were waiting anxiously and erupted in delight when their guests arrived. Party time!

Most of the animals hadn't met Ma, only Copycat, and the birds, but they all had their own ideas. All were right in their own way. She came to the front porch in a sun dress, partially covered with a gingham check apron. She had the eyes of age, eyes that had seen much, yet she offered a broad and welcoming smile. She waved at the arrivals with a spatula in hand.

Ma liked Agnes and Theo and Xander almost

immediately. "I have heard about your escapades. Please make yourself at home. There is a cooler of beer over there," another wave with her spatula, "and I have wine inside. Come in Agnes and I'll get you a glass and we can chat."

Agnes did not need to be asked twice and followed Ma inside. The smell of apple pie and blueberry crisp was sublime. Agnes felt right at home.

Outside, the men all did the handshake and bro-hug thing while Fern held court with all the animals, including Geppetto and Nancy who had just arrived.

"What's cooking?" Theo said as he sniffed the air.

"I'm glad you asked," Carl said with a huge grin. "Look over here." He led the men over to the side of the yard and motioned with a beer can in hand. "Ta-Da!"

"What is that?" Xander wanted to know.

"That there," Elvis informed them, "is a sixty-pound pig. I shot it myself."

They stared at a metal lined hot-box, filled with smoking hardwood embers and a dressed pig with an apple stuck in its mouth. It was turning slowly on a motorized rotisserie.

Theo and Xander didn't know what to say, having never actually seen anything like this.

Carl broke the silence. "It's been going low and slow for about seven hours. It's going to be super good."

"Why is there an apple in its mouth?" Xander asked.

"That's to prop his mouth open so the hot air can circulate inside while it's cooking," said Carl.

"And, to let internal gasses escape," Elvis added.

Carl looked at him. "Yeah, gasses."

Theo and Xander nodded as if all this made sense.

"We also have some brisket over here for the grill, and

Ma's got baked beans, and coleslaw all lined up for us. You guys want a beer?" Carl offered. "We got them on ice right here."

"Sure," said a very pleased Xander.

Theo glanced around and hesitated before speaking. "You know what? I was wondering if you had a shovel I could borrow?"

Nobody moved or said anything. They all knew what the shovel was for.

"Fern," Elvis called. "Come over here for a second."

Fern looked up to see Elvis waving a hand at her and made her way over to the men. Carl went over to the shed to get a shovel for Theo.

Elvis was solemn in his tone out of respect for Theo. "Fern, I want you to take Mr. Bobnoggin on the boat." He caught himself and addressed Carl. "Soop, we got gas in that thing?"

"Yeah, I filled it myself," Carl answered, handing Theo a shovel.

Back to Elvis. "Fern, go and get Ma's rifle without her seeing you. Mr. Bobnoggin has some unfinished business."

Without a word, Fern sneaked into the house and came back with Ma's gun. "Who's coming on the boat?"

"I think Copycat and Figaro will want to pay their respects," Theo said. "Geppetto can fly along with us if he wants."

"Okay," Fern nodded. "I'll bring Pretty with us too. We can stay in the boat while you do what you need to do."

"Thank you, Fern. Thank you." Then to the men: "I expect to be back within the hour."

"Perfect," Elvis said. "And, I expect you'll be hungry when you get here."

Carl caught Fern by the arm. "You be careful, Fern. You

know where you're going?"

"I know exactly where I'm going."

Xander stayed with the boys while Ripley and Digby loitered about with Yogi, Diesel, and Nancy, none of them saying much.

It was a relatively quiet and unhurried ride in the boat, across flat water, the greenish-gray color of leftover guacamole, to the place where chaos had visited upon the swamp and gunfire had filled the air.

"This is it, Theo. Right through there about a hundred yards," Fern said, pointing with her chin. "I'll wait here with Pretty."

Theo got out, shovel in hand, and, along with Copycat and Figaro, they made their way to the place where he had done battle with The Big Bad. "This is where it went down," he said to Figaro as they emerged onto the clearing.

The three of them were heart-struck by the scene. The monster alligator was gone. Pulled back into the water by whatever creature had the strength. All that was left was a bloody mess at the edge of the water. A large black vulture was there, standing over the body of Julius.

"Hello," Theo said.

"Hello. My name is Delroy," the bird said to the man. "I am a close friend of Fern and Pretty." Delroy looked at Copycat and Figaro, huddled together. "And Copycat."

"I'm pleased to meet you, Delroy."

Theo's eyes traveled to Julius, then back to Delroy. "Why are you here?" he addressed the vulture.

"I'm here to watch over Julius. I don't want any animal to disrespect his body. I've been standing guard because I knew you would come."

"How did you know that?" Theo was puzzled.

"Because you are a good human, and for whatever reason, good humans bury their loved ones."

Theo thought for a moment. "How do you know I am a good human?"

"Geppetto told me," Delroy said, before lifting off skyward.

Theo set about the sweaty, but necessary, business of digging a grave for Julius. He worked at it, digging deep, and quietly sobbing all the while. Copycat and Figaro could hardly watch. Deeper and deeper went Theo, until he could not dig anymore.

Fern told Pretty to stay by the boat so she could sneak a peek through the brush. Unseen and silent, a Seminole of the Wind Clan, she watched.

A warm breath on her face, a tickle of whiskers on her cheek. Fern knew who was beside her. "Hello, Nika," she whispered. "What are you doing here?"

"Watching your back. I will always have your back."

"And I will always have yours", Fern started to say, but Nika was gone. A ghost in the swamp.

The burying done and a mound heaped over Julius's grave, Theo thought to say something about his friend but hadn't the words. He, Copycat, and Figaro said their silent goodbyes.

I'LL BE THERE FOR YOU

ELVIS WAS STARING at the grill, unsure when to throw the brisket on the heat. He was mentally calculating the time it would take for Theo to return and the time it would take for Soop to do his thing to the pig - now resting on a makeshift plywood table.

Carl was unnecessarily sharpening his trusty blade on a whetstone with unconcealed glee. Time to carve the beast. With an over-sized fork in his left hand and his super sharp knife in the other, he set about the business of disassembling the pig the way only a southern boy could.

Xander was watching Carl with great interest when he said, "I'll be back in a minute." Soop didn't even hear him, so fully absorbed in his reverie.

Xander went into the kitchen to see Agnes and Ma, tending to pies and pastries on the counter and table, and yapping away with smiles on their faces.

"I see you two have been busy," Xander smiled right along with them. "This will be a feast to remember."

"I think you're right!" Ma and Agnes said together.

Xander lifted his nose and made an *mmm* sound. "I can hardly wait for some of that apple pie." He looked out the kitchen window to see the boat being pulled up on the bank and Theo and Fern clambering out. "It looks like they are back."

"Who?" Agnes asked.

"Fern and Theo."

The two women exchanged a glance. "Did they go somewhere?"

"Never mind. I'll let you get back to your baking." He made to leave but turned back in interest. "What's that you are making now?"

"Shoofly pie. You'll love it."

Xander and the two Pettigrew brothers met Theo and Fern at the boat. Pretty, Figaro, and Copycat were already making their way back to the other animals. Geppetto had since returned from his aerial surveillance.

"Everything go okay?" Elvis wanted to know.

"Everything is fine," Theo said, as he nodded a thank you to Elvis and Carl.

"Well, good. Time to eat, I'm starving." Carl was incandescent with anticipation.

With a little help from Agnes, Ma had set up a folding card table beside the picnic table and some lawn chairs along with it. Seating for seven humans. There were mismatched melamine plates, equally mismatched cutlery, and red Solo cups along with a small mountain of paper napkins. It was heavenly.

Dinner was a hodge-podge of family-style and buffet. The roasted pig had been pulled by the expert hand of Carl and was on a giant serving platter next to the plywood table where he had done his work. There were dinner rolls and BBQ sauce and huge trays of baked beans and coleslaw.

Carl had saved a hunk of prized cheek meat for the guest of honor and placed it in a small bowl. "Theo, would you ask Copycat to come over here for a taste?"

Theo leaned over to look in the bowl. "What is that?"

"Cheek meat. The best part of the whole pig."

Theo called over to Copycat who dutifully ignored him. "C'mon Copycat. They say it's even better than ice cream."

"Ice cream?"

Copycat wandered over to the table, not wanting to appear too anxious, and looked into the bowl Carl had put down before him. A sniff. A lick. A nibble. A big bite. Pretty soon it was all gone. Carl was delighted with the five-star review Copycat was apparently giving him.

After they had all eaten like gluttons, Elvis and Soop cleared the dishes so that Ma could do her *big reveal*. She and Agnes carried out two apple pies and a blueberry crisp. Who's going to eat all this?

All sated and happy, the conversation fell into a lull. There was some talk about politics, but not much. Some talk about the weather, but not much. Theo thought this would be a good time to tell the Pettigrews that he was going back *up north* in the morning. He had had enough adventure to last a lifetime and he wanted to get back to Nicky. They had all known it was coming but had come to enjoy the excitement that Theo had brought with him. Mostly they were thrilled to have met a man who could communicate with animals the way Fern could. Fern was not alone.

"I want you to know that you are always welcome

here, Mr. Bobnoggin," Ma said. "And you, Agnes," she turned to her new friend, "I expect you to be a regular visitor."

Agnes beamed. "You know I will."

Xander glanced around at all the leftover food. "What will you do with all this?"

"All what?" Elvis asked.

"This food. You have a ton of it."

"Well, Ma will make sandwiches for Theo to take on the ride back to Illinois," Carl said, before continuing, "The rest, me and Elvis will take into town tomorrow. There's a homeless shelter for vets there, and we like to bring them a good feast now and then."

Xander thought about this. "Would you mind if I tag along? Maybe thank them for their service?"

Carl nodded. "Yup, sure thing. Tomorrow after work. We'll come and pick you up."

"I'd really appreciate that."

"Xander?

"Yeah?"

"Can I get a ride in that golf cart you got?"

Fern excused herself and strolled over to where the animals were gathered. The squirrels were saying some goodbyes and encouraging Diesel and Pretty to come for a visit sometime at the sanctuary in Theo's backyard in Illinois. It was a sincere invitation, though they all knew it would never happen. Probably.

Xander sauntered over to join them. "Hey, Fern, you have a minute?"

"Sure."

"Maybe we could speak privately."

"Here *is* private." She looked around at the animals

assembled around her. "They aren't going to understand a word you say."

Xander raised his eyebrows. "I suppose you're right."

"Before you say anything, Xander, I want to tell you how much respect I have for the way you had Theo's back. You were there for him when he needed you. That tells me a lot about you."

"I appreciate that, Fern. But there is a lot you still don't know about me." Xander sat down on the ground and crossed his legs. "I come from a very dark place. Afghanistan has been at war, in one form or another, since before anyone can remember. Over the years I have had the privilege of working closely with the United States military. I have a good idea of how they operate. I met many good men and I also met with some questionable leadership. Those in power will do anything to gain even the slightest tactical advantage. Rightly so, I guess. At least to a point." Xander paused for a moment.

Fern wondered where this was going.

"I am going to tell you the same thing I told Theo, because, like him, you have a special gift. Please keep your wits about you at all times, Fern. Be aware of who might be watching you and try not to put your particular talents on public display. You are obviously safe here with the Pettigrews, but there are some who would want to take advantage of you."

"I'm not quite sure what you mean."

"Fern, there are those who would wish to harness your gift. Or, at least try. Maybe the federal government?" Xander suggested.

Fern cocked her head a notch to the side. Confused. "What would the federal government want with me?"

Xander exhaled a deep breath. "They would seek to

weaponize you."

A blank stare.

"Fern, I don't want to scare you. Just caution you. If the CIA became aware of either you or Theo, they would come calling. So would the FBI, so would military intelligence, and so would anyone even remotely associated with our national defense apparatus."

"This is hard to believe."

"Trust me. A human who could communicate with any animal, anywhere, would be an intelligence-gathering asset without compare. They would use you and Theo whether you liked it or not."

Fern was still trying to figure this out. "Okay. Well, thanks for the advice." She didn't know what else to say.

"Just don't advertise your powers to the world and you will be fine." Xander smiled a friendly smile, hoping he hadn't upset the girl.

Fern, Pretty, and Diesel, along with the boys and Ma, were grouped around Theo's Audi, watching Agnes carefully place generous helpings of leftovers in the back seat. After the animals all said their goodbyes, it was time for the humans to do the same.

Agnes insisted she would be a frequent visitor to Ma's house and would bring cookies next time. She gave Ma and Fern a hug, telling Fern she would have lemonade or iced tea for her and the boys whenever they might be around Riverside Estates.

Xander extended the same offer of hospitality and shook hands with Elvis and Carl, reminding them he would see them tomorrow for a ride on the golf cart and a visit to the homeless shelter.

Theo's turn. "You never know when I might plan

another road trip. This won't be the last time I come to see Agnes." He turned to Fern. "Listen to me, please. Listen to what I am telling you. If you need anything, you call me. Ma and the boys all have my number, and they will take good care of you. But, if you need to talk about, you know, things with animals, I'll be there for you."

Pretty piped up. "She knows, Mr. Bobnoggin. She knows."

IT GAVE HIM JOY

KARL GOT OFF the elevator on the executive floor. "Good morning, Marcy."

"Good morning, Mr. Snell."

He was going to like this. He walked over to the doors of his father's office, Marcy beating him to it where she opened the door for him. He went inside the large office and looked around before sitting down in the *big chair* like he owned the place. Which he sort of did at this point.

"Marcy, please have someone bring up all the things from my old office, thanks."

"Yes sir, Mr. Snell."

"Marcy?"

"Yes?"

"How much do I pay you?"

She wanted to say *not enough* but kept her mouth shut.

"Well, whatever it is, call HR and tell them I just gave you a ten percent raise."

"Yes sir, Mr. Snell." Day one was off to a good start.

Karl was tipped back in his full-grain leather chair, feet on his desk, thinking about the Porsche he was going to buy. Marcy got a nice raise but he had given himself a nicer one. A lot nicer.

His desk phone chirped. "Mr. Snell?"

"Yes?"

"I have a Mr. Bruno Fischer on the line."

"Put him through."

"Hi, Bruno. How's the lawyering business?"

"Hello, Karl. Are you enjoying yourself in the Big Boy office?"

"Immensely.

"Well, you would be a hero around here but nobody knows it."

"Really?"

"Yeah. Because of your timely information, an arson plot was foiled. But you already know that."

"Yeah. So why are you calling?

"Detective Donovan? Jay Donovan? He wants to know where I got the tip. Do you want me to tell him or not?"

"Sure. Go ahead and tell him. It doesn't matter now. I just didn't want him to know ahead of time."

"Why is that?"

"Because he knows my father. They had done some *business* together." Karl said. "Anyway, It's done now. I didn't want to see the animal clinic burn down. Or Bobnoggin's house for that matter. I'm not all bad, you know. I have a heart."

"Yeah. A heart of stone. You gave up your sister and father."

"I did my civic duty, Bruno, so don't give me any of that family crap. They are arsonists who got caught. Period."

"If that's what you need to tell yourself, have it your

way, Karl. I'll go ahead and let Donovan know it was you. You should expect a call from the local news."

Karl began snooping around in his new office. He peeked and poked at a shelf here and a drawer there. He would have to re-decorate. He didn't like all those framed photos of his father, shaking hands with people he didn't recognize. And this carpet? Really?

His desk phone chirped again. "Mr. Snell?

"Yes?"

"I have Emma Taylor from the Ashburn Free Press on the line."

Karl took the call.

No, *shucks*, he wasn't a hero. We all have a responsibility to do the right thing, even when it is difficult. He hoped that his sister would get the help she obviously needs. He was heartbroken that his father was involved. He will work to restore the family name and the company's reputation. Happy to be of service to the community.

Karl's day just could not stop getting better and better. He asked Marcy if she had the combination to his father's safe and she did! This one knows everything. I'll have to be careful with her.

Karl was counting the stacks of money he had piled on his desk, doing the math and singing a song. He felt like a drug kingpin in the movies as he stuffed it back into the safe. What was his father doing with all that cash? Then it occurred to him - it was getaway money. Sorry, Dad, you didn't get away fast enough. Don't worry, I'll take care of everything while you are in prison.

* * *

Karl's head was spinning. With the Porsche (build your own) website still on his screen, he clicked open a new browser window and googled something about how to change the combination on a wall safe. Call the manufacturer. Lots to do. Busy, busy. He pulled open a desk drawer to look for some paper and a pen and found the necktie his father had taken from him. He had forgotten about that. I'll have that back thanks, he almost said aloud.

He picked up his phone. "Marcy, do we have anyone in-house who can scout locations for the Cuban chicken guys? I can't do that anymore. Too busy."

"Let me check, Mr. Snell."

Less than thirty seconds later, Karl's phone chirped yet again. "Yes?"

"I have Mr. Paul Gentry from the Ashburn Golf and Country Club on the line."

"Okay, put him through. No, wait. Keep him on hold for about half a minute first, just for fun, then put him through."

"Yes, Mr. Snell."

This was turning into the greatest day of Karl's life. He might have to go back to Lonny's for another steak tonight. Thirty seconds were up.

"Hello, Paul."

"Surprise, surprise, Snell. It's your old pal, Paul Gentry."

"I know. My personal assistant told me. Why are you calling?"

"I wanted to congratulate you. Your sister is in the hospital and your father is behind bars. How does it feel?"

"It feels terrible, Paul. Nobody wants to see a family member suffer. I just couldn't sit back and let the animal clinic and Bobnoggin's house burn."

"Wrong, Snell. Wrong again. You should have let it happen and we would be talking about a buyout and building tennis courts on that land right now. You should have burned it down yourself last year when you had the chance. And now you've screwed it all up again."

"I had a moral obligation, Gentry." Karl paused for a beat. "I'm sorry, Paul. Could you hold for just a moment?" Karl put Gentry on hold, not because he had to, not because he had another call, but because he felt like it. Opportunities this rich in entertainment value don't come around very often.

After close to a minute, Karl could see that Gentry was still there. The little red light blinked on line one. "Hello? Sorry about that, Paul. You still there?"

"Yes, I am here."

"So, anything else Gentry?"

"No. I just wanted to tell you that you are still the loser you have always been. You can't stop screwing up. You are a loser, Snell. Please kill yourself."

Karl was grinning from ear to ear. He didn't have the chance to respond, as Paul Gentry had hung up. That's okay. Karl was thrilled to hear Gentry so angry. It gave him joy.

Karl did go to Lonny's that night. He had invited Marcy to come along but she declined. No fool, that Marcy, thought Karl as he sipped his martini at the bar. This place is nice. I might have to become a regular.

He sipped and people-watched and mused to himself. Why has nobody quite figured this out? Maybe his lawyer did - Bruno obviously had his suspicions. But nobody seemed to fully understand that he could not possibly care less about the animal clinic or Bobnoggin's house. He just did not care. What he *did* care about was having his sister and his father out of the way. Gerda had handed it to him on a silver platter when she told him of her plans to commit arson. All Karl had to do was make a phone call and wait for Gerda to walk straight into his trap. The cherry on top was Gerda, singing like a canary to the police, and implicating their father. And then his father, in an absolute cognitive meltdown, put him in charge of the company while being dragged away in cuffs. In his wildest dreams, Karl didn't think he could have planned it any better.

I WILL SEE YOU AGAIN

IT WAS TIME to leave. Bags had been packed and loaded into Theo's SUV, along with lots of bottled water, snacks, supplies, and some ice cream in a cooler for Copycat. Theo had charged the Audi the night before so they could get a good start. They had gathered in the driveway for the goodbye session that nobody wanted. There was no joy in Mudville that morning.

Dante and Elliot were there, Geppetto and Nancy, Xander and Yogi. Theodore and the three squirrels. Agnes held Copycat in her arms. All were acutely aware of Julius's absence.

The Gators-Be-Gone van had been touched-up with paint to read: "Elvis and Soop" and then below that "+ Fern" which had delighted Fern to no end. They had to work, just like most people, and rolled into Riverside Estates. They passed Agnes's house without stopping. "Give them their space," Elvis advised. "We said goodbye last night."

Carl nodded in agreement. Fern just looked out the window at the congregation on the driveway. She was going to miss them.

Rip, Fig, and Dig were hustled into the back seat. Copycat was reluctant to leave Agnes's embrace but eventually did so of his own accord. Yogi stood at the open car door and said his goodbyes to the squirrels as Theo and Xander exchanged a full-on hug, complete with hearty back-slaps.

Theo had saved Agnes for last. When they embraced it was only love. Warm and tender and gentle. No words were exchanged.

Theo turned to the big black crow perched on a low branch of a live oak. "Let's go, Geppetto."

Geppetto cocked his head at an angle, sneaking a peek at Nancy beside him. "I'm not leaving, Theo. I want to stay here with Nancy."

Theo held the eyes of the bird. There was no point in discussing it with Geppetto. There would be no negotiation. When Geppetto spoke, it was truth and that was all there was to it. "I'm happy for you Geppetto. We will all miss you very much, but we will always know you for what you are. A peerless friend and a crow to be trusted."

Figaro could hear all of this from the backseat and bolted out onto the driveway. Geppetto, out of respect for the little red squirrel with the mightiest of hearts, fluttered down to the driveway to see his friend. "I will miss you, Fig."

"I will miss you too, you beady-eyed fowl. You haven't seen the last of me."

"Let's hope so, Fig. In the meantime, I will watch over Agnes, check in with Yogi, and patrol the skies with Nancy. There will be another Big Bad, we just don't know who or what yet. I promise you, Fig, I will be here waiting for him."

"And what will you do then, Geppetto," Figaro asked.

"I will find Fern and Pretty. They will find Delroy and the panther. We will talk to Yogi and Xander. Together we will hunt it and kill it. For Julius."

"And when the next one comes along?"

"We will hunt that one too."

"I'm not sure you will ever finish, Geppetto. There will always be another. Vengeance will become hollow."

"When that day comes, I will stop."

Figaro inched forward to give the crow a snuggle, before scampering back into the backseat.

Geppetto leaped up, with a clumsy flap, to settle on Theo's shoulder.

"Take care, Theo. Give my best wishes to Hendrix and to Doc Nicky."

"I will Geppetto. I will see you again. I promise. I don't know how I know this, but I do. I can feel it in my bones."

Florida turned into Georgia and then to Tennessee. Theo was determined to drive straight through. With just the three squirrels and a cat, the trip was relatively stress-free. Theo had the music turned low and the animals mostly napped. There were vehicle charging breaks and potty breaks, but the trip was smooth. Adrenaline kicked in by the time he got to Indiana. There would be no stopping now. He had driven through the night and was thinking of nothing but Nicky. He could hear her calling for him. I'm coming, Nicky. I'm coming home.

THE WISDOM OF AN OWL

THEY WERE LINED up in Theo's driveway. Doctor Nichole Florentine was front and center, Riley, and Cierra on her left, and Buster the rabbit with Oscar the skunk on her right. Hendrix was on the eave of Theo's garage roof, just behind Doc Nicky.

When Theo pulled into the driveway, pandemonium erupted in his backseat. He knew enough to open the backseat door as quickly as possible for Rip, Fig, Dig and Copycat, lest they shred his leather upholstery in their excitement.

Three squirrels, a cat, a skunk, and a rabbit, all began running around in circles on the driveway, tumbling over one another in their joy.

Theo and Nicky embraced and would not let go for minutes. I'm so glad you are home. I'm so glad to be home. I love you. I missed you. I love you too. Both of them whispering through short breaths, holding back tears.

It was Hendrix, with the wisdom of an owl, who let the human emotions run and run as if they wouldn't stop, before he said: "Hello, Theo. Where is Julius? Where is

Geppetto? You left with them and have come back without them."

ONE MORE BOX TO CHECK

KARL WAS REVIEWING a list of potential in-house candidates for the job of driving all over Florida, looking for a likely spot for the Cubans to put one of their chicken restaurants. His old job. The problem was, he knew the Cubans to be smart, entrepreneurial, and not prone to being fed a load of real-estate hyperbole. He needed to make a good hire.

His feet were up on his desk. Leaning in his chair, he was taking a break from staring at a screen. His mind wandered. He had needs to satisfy. He had boxes to check. He was a man who would not be outdone. He did a quick review of recent successes. Gerda in the hospital, injured but alive, soon to be imprisoned. Check. His father being held without bail on felony charges. (Apparently, the courts felt he was a flight risk. No kidding.) Check. He was sitting in the corner office, in what used to be his father's chair, fully in charge of the Precept Realty and Development Group. Check. Gentry at the golf club *up north* was as mad as a hatter. The more Gentry hated him, the greater the success. Check. He was viewed by some in

Ashburn as, incredibly, a civic hero. His name held in high regard. Screw Gentry. Check.

But something felt missing. His brand spanking new Porsche had been ordered, yet Karl felt unfulfilled. He thought some more and knew what it was. Theo and his friends had humiliated him. Theo was back in Illinois, but Agnes and her huckleberry friends were still here. Those two swamp assholes stole his money and had zip-tied him, and carted him around on the back of that stinking trailer. And then there was the girl. The girl with the stupid iguana she would talk to. She would talk to birds, dogs, whatever. Just like Theo. Yeah. Just like Theo. Huh. This little hole inside of Karl needed to be filled. And now it occurred to him how to do it. He had one more box to check.

BE PROUD

THEO WAS HAPPY to be back at the patio table in his backyard and to be spending the evening with Nicky. He had produced a beautiful Batard Montrachet from inside when he sat to pour Nicky a glass of wine. But his happiness was tempered with a melancholy hanging over him

"I have a difficult thing ahead of me, Nicky. I need to speak to Marcus and Evander. They need to hear about Julius from me."

Nicky sipped at her wine. *Delicious*, she thought. "I know, Theo. It will be rough." Another sip of wine. "I respect you for your courage and your wanting to do the right thing." She paused for a beat. "Although, I think I would expect nothing less of you, my sweet."

"Hendrix took it well, sort of. Oscar and Buster, maybe not so much. I think Hendrix is hurting, but just won't show it."

"He *can't* show it," Nicky tried to say as softly as she could. "Hendrix is in pain, but he simply can't show it. He's an owl."

Theo and Nicky spent the rest of the evening drinking wine and not talking. The way that those in love don't need to talk all the time, they were happy to just be in each other's company. Just being.

At a very late hour, Doc Nicky declared that she was responsible for opening the clinic in the morning, and simply had to go to bed.

"Will you go home, or stay here with me?"

"Tonight I will go home to my place, Theo. You have things to do." Nicky's eyes twinkled. "Tomorrow night, mister, tomorrow." And then, perhaps, for many nights to come, she thought but didn't say.

The evening sun had lost its grasp, yielding to a sliver of moon. Theo sat in his chair at his table and waited in the dark. And waited. He knew Hendrix would come, sooner or later.

At some point, well after midnight, when bad things happen, when darkness lets free the little devils of the night, when the *only* sounds are the sounds of those who were hunted and caught; Hendrix landed on the patio table to face Theo.

"I am sorry, Hendrix. I know you want to blame me. There was nothing I could do."

"I know, Theo. It's all right. What do you want from me? You are not sitting here in the middle of the night for nothing."

"I want you to find Marcus and Evander. They need to hear the news from me. I will meet them on their territory, on the golf course, wherever. It doesn't matter.

Hendrix flew off to make the arrangements and returned to Theo to give him the news. "Just walk through the creek, onto the golf course, and stay put. They will find you."

Theo did as instructed. He sloshed across Sycamore Creek and onto the golf course in the black of night. He knew Hendrix was up high, watching.

Theo sat down, submissive, respectful of territory, in the middle of the 17th fairway and waited for the twin coyotes to come. It was not long before Marcus appeared. And then Evander. The two sons of Julius.

Theo told them of the extraordinary bravery of their father. The one-eyed coyote who had, against all odds, fought and won against all manner of beast, all manner of foe. A lifetime of valor. The coyote who had so improbably befriended a house cat and a red squirrel. Theo told Marcus and Evander of The Big Bad. The monster that Julius had faced down. The cat he had saved, the demon whose face he had spat upon. The unmitigated loyalty that was embedded within him.

"Be proud Marcus. Evander, you as well. Your father's legend will live forever."

"Thank you, Mr. Bobnoggin," Marcus said respectfully. "I appreciate what you are doing for all of us."

Evander, the one who rarely spoke, added: "We are here if you should ever need us. Just as our father would have been."

STAY ON THE PORCH

STARING OUT HIS office window, much in the same way that his father did, Karl watched the planes fly in and out of Orlando International Airport. He was considering the implications of his plan. The long-term consequences.

He liked this *hero* thing. Sure, money would always be the most important thing to him, but this whole *hero* thing was gaining traction. If he could be a local hero in little old Ashburn, Illinois, why couldn't he be a national hero? Why think *small* when you could think *big*? If you can't run with the big dogs, then stay on the porch.

He knew of something that would be a matter of national security. He knew of something that could be of *extreme* value to the country, and Karl was nothing, if not a patriot. He knew what would be an intelligence nightmare for our enemies. He knew of something that would put him in history books! He, Karl Snell, knew of humans who could talk to animals!

Karl, convinced he was doing the right thing, sat at his desk and googled the phone number for the Director of the

CIA. There wasn't one - a number that is. There were a few weird numbers that were of no value, but you could not call the Director of the CIA directly. Apparently, if there was a GIGANTIC NATIONAL SECURITY ISSUE, you had to fill out some sort of online form. The (OPA) Office of Public Affairs would look at it. Maybe. Whatever. Karl Snell was not going to fill out a form for some minimum wage clerk to decide whether or not it was worthy. This was not good.

Screw the CIA. Let's try the FBI.

This was a little easier. Sort of. A lot of numbers and a lot of voicemail prompts. An online tip form. "You may not get a reply to your submission due to the large volume of submissions the FBI receives…"

Karl was nonplussed. He had critical information about something that could be used for the defense of America! Nobody seemed to care.

A NEW ARRIVAL

THREE MONTHS LATER, the early October sun was of premium quality. The evening sky was cobalt blue, and an hour before sunset, when apricot and peach would appear on the horizon, she would slowly surrender to the night.

Theo and Nicky were happily planted in their seats at the backyard patio table. Buster, the ridiculously overweight rabbit, had enthusiastically assumed His Lordship over the backyard after the passing of Julius. Running to and fro, he would issue edicts at random, to which all would pledge fealty and then laugh their heads off behind his back. Yes, my Lord!What fun. Hendrix would watch from on high. Rip, Fig, and Dig would join in. There was nothing, if not love, that filled the air.

Theo looked up and face-signaled to Hendrix. A look and a nod and a cock of his head. The owl knew this language and floated down, to the backyard.

Theo sauntered over toward Hendrix. Cool, like. Nothing to see here. Nothing happening here.

Hendrix knew everything. It is not known how, but it is fact. In the Backyard Chronicles of the strangest of strange, the oddest of odd, Hendrix knew everything. Always.

"Go and get the boys."

That was all Theo had to say.

Hendrix landed at the end of the patio table a solid half hour later.

Marcus and Evander, Julius's boys, approached from the end of the backyard that edged against the creek.

The squirrels, Buster, and Oscar were there too. Apparently, an army of chipmunks had heard also, that there was going to be an announcement.

Theo looked at Nicky and Nicky looked at Theo. The electricity could light up Paris.

"What's going on?" Ripley wanted to know.

"Well, shall we tell them?" Theo smiled at Nicky.

"You will have to," Nicky grinned. "They won't understand me."

Theo sighed. Here goes. "Ripley, come here, please. I want you beside me."

Ripley complied.

"Well, everyone, there is going to be a new arrival, a new member of our backyard alliance."

"Who?" Figaro asked with characteristic impatience.

"Doc Nicky is pregnant."

"What? What? What?" The animals said variously.

"We are going to have a baby."

The animals went wild. Not Marcus and Evander, of course, but the rest of them began running in circles with excitement, crashing into each other and bouncing off to do it again.

"Wait! Wait!" It was Ripley, the mom squirrel who

wanted to ask a mom-type question. "Is it going to be a boy or a girl?"

The antics came to a stop as they all listened for the answer. Theo and Nicky moved a little closer together.

"It's a boy!"

The festivities resumed. Chaos reigned in the backyard.

"I'm so happy, I literally can't even!" Digby shouted.

"I know! Same!" Figaro shouted back.

"Wait! Wait!" Ripley again. "Do you have a name picked out?"

"Yeah," Figaro and Digby said together. "What is his name?"

"Theo Junior?" Buster suggested.

Theo gave Nicky a squeeze. "They want to know what we will name our son."

"So, tell them." Nicky was grinning ear to ear.

"Marcus, Evander, come a little closer please." They did.

"We have decided on a name. A special name."

"Well, what is it?" They all wanted to know.

Theo smiled. "Julius. Our son will be Julius Bobnoggin."

Tears flowed like Niagra Falls. Copycat jumped onto Theo's lap, and on the brink of lost composure, said: "Julius Bobnoggin."

Marcus and Evander both lowered their heads in a nod to Theo. Thank you. A noble name indeed.

EPILOGUE

KARL SNELL HAD become a regular at Lonny's. Flashing his plastic and enjoying his martinis. The bartender had to cut him off more than a few times, not wanting Karl to kill himself, or anyone else, while driving home. I think maybe you've had enough, Mr. Snell. Karl took it in stride, knowing the bartender was probably right.

The new carpeting had been installed in his office and an underling had been hired to scout locations for the Cubans. The new guy was doing well. A good hire. They already had two locations under contract. Making money. Gerda was out of the hospital and awaiting trial under home confinement. Herman was also under home confinement with the Judge denying him access to the internet and cell phone service. TV only, plus a closely monitored telephone land-line to call his lawyer. No visitors except legal counsel. He had been given strict instruction to not, under any circumstances, contact Karl. That would be witness tampering.

* * *

Everything seemed to be going well for Karl, but he still had a simmering hatred for Theodore Bobnoggin. He thought about this as he lounged on the leather sofa in his office. He had been waiting patiently for someone to get back to him. Somebody from the federal government. He had filled out the online forms and left voice mail messages. The FBI, the CIA. Even the Pentagon. Nothing. He just could not believe they wouldn't want to hear what he had to say. The value in having an asset that could communicate with animals was, in his mind, incalculable.

Having worked himself into a state, Karl had had enough. The feds weren't going to give him anything anyway. Maybe a thank you, that's about it. But there would be no payoff for him other than the pleasure of causing a major problem for Bobnoggin and that girl from the swamp. No. Screw them. There had to be a way to *monetize* this.

It hit him like a hammer. I know who will listen to me. I also know these same people will pay me a lot of money for my information. He jumped up and practically *ran* to his desk.

He googled the phone number for the Chinese Embassy in Washington, DC.

Printed in Great Britain
by Amazon